Beyond the Edge

SHANE W. SHELTON

Beyond the Edge

By Shane Wesley Shelton

Believing Magic Books

First U.S. edition 2014

ISBN: 978-1-941570-37-1

DRM provided by Boker and Amazon Digital Service

Grammatical line editing and read through proofing by:
Sherri McDougald – English major at University of North Florida

Cover artwork purchased on Shutter Stock

Believing Magic Books
13 Kingfish Avenue
Ponte Vedra Beach, Florida 32082
Visit us at **www.believingmagic.com**

Chapters

Beyond the Edge

Someone shoved me from behind.

"Get out'a the way townie girl!"

I didn't turn around to see who it was, even though I wanted to do that and whole lot more. I'd have been trampled if I tried. Gritting my teeth and hating my life, I kept moving at the pace of traffic. There were only four hundred of us in this outdated, red brick asylum that passed for a school in the godforsaken hellhole of Preston County, PA. All the students were squeezed together as we shoved our way down the narrow main hall that made four hundred feel like four thousand, every last one of us headed to the auditorium for a mandatory morning prayer of all things. Mandatory prayer! In a public school! Blatant evidence that I was in a religious, hillbilly backwater masquerading as civilization. Only half of the kids around me even bothered to carry books, and at least half were wearing the same clothes as what they'd worn yesterday, or the day before. Some had the same clothes on now as what they started out the week with, though it was hard to tell with the townies as all the boys wore blue overalls paired with long sleeved blue undershirts and the townie girls wore long sleeved, faded, ankle length dresses in one or two styles. No flare. The 'Townies' were easy to pick out from the kids who were more modern arrivals. Teens whose parents had bought the only cheap dirt left in the state, consigning their children to grow up in this pitiful existence, and dooming themselves to an hour long drive every day both ways to Barstow or an hour and a half commute in the opposite direction to reach Allentown. The name brand clothes and the superior airs of the commuter kids were all muted and not thrown in anyone's faces because the keepers of this zoo were all locals and the commuter kids knew it. And now, so did I.

It was Friday. Filthy Friday at Preston PA High. Time felt skewed. It felt like I'd been here a thousand years already, walking these halls again and again and I'd only been here one week. Nine days since my mother rushed here and took possession of her parents home, six since the burial. I say burial because there had been no funeral. Six actual days spent in this school. I arrived on a filthy Friday and the smell of the place nearly made me shit myself when I first walked through the doors. On Monday the smell was better. At first I thought it was the weekend

---

and the cleaning crews getting crazy with bleach, opening windows and airing the place out, but now I knew what it was, and what it wasn't. I also knew that every window in this fire trap was nailed shut. The stagnant air and the 'feel' of the place built through the week to this current level. Filthy Friday. It was a mix of boy sweat, cow shit and coal dust carried in on boots and trampled into the ground. It was the disgust put off by the commuter kids and the hate radiating from the townies that felt that their home was being invaded, the fear of both groups, and above all the hopelessness. The town kids were from backward, religious families who worked farms or delved coal mines and they knew that Preston was where they'd work and live and one day die, just like their mothers and fathers, grandmothers, grandfathers, great grandmothers, great grandfathers and so on. Most of the townie boys would already be underground if they wouldn't have made eighteen the legal age to start killing yourself with black lung. The commuter kids who, like me, had seen the world in color now either walked with the bitterness of that loss carved into their faces or staggered down the drab halls with vacant expressions, utterly broken and reduced to grey eyed, soul sucked podlings decked out by their parents in laundered clothes whose bright colors did nothing for the colorless teens who wore them.

I looked around as we trudged en mass past beady eyed teachers who stood in doorways glaring like predator fish eyeing a bait ball. Occasionally one of the big, beefy men would reach out and grab a student by the arm and yank them out of the steam, calling him/her into classes or pushing them up against lockers. We couldn't get away. Even the big, mean, townie boys were trapped in a way. Helpless fish in the stream beneath the eyes of the teachers. Victims. I had no idea what was said in hushed whispers or what happened in those classrooms, but I'd probably find out soon. Whatever protective, new kid radiation I had was just about spent, especially since I was practically a townie myself, just one who'd been misplaced for a very long time thanks to my mother. The office received my file from my old school in Florida on Monday and promptly spilled the beans that I'd been a student of 'alternative sexual orientation'. As if being an outed newbie wasn't enough ammo for the firing squad, I'd already heard the townie kids talking about my mother and our family, only they called us by my grandmother's last name. DeLaCroix. Every kid in school had heard by now that the only shopping my mother had done was to the liquor store and back. All these teachers and the parents of the townie students grew up with my mother and her older sister, my Aunt Fay, and they knew our family. I saw them grouped together, whispering about me. About us. Which was strange, because they knew more about my family than I did. That day at the funeral home was the first and only time I'd seen my grandmother. Only dead. Only in a box. Never alive. Only gray. Scowling. Eternally. It seemed to fit the place, and my luck.

Larry Opar and his thugs told me yesterday that today would be the day they'd 'sanctify me'. Even dared me to tell a teacher or the principal. Larry suggested, with what seemed genuine concern, that I not tell Mr. Ronicker, saying that if he caught wind I was fresh meat he'd keep me for himself. I'd stood there in the hall pressed up against the lockers with that bastards two goons pawing at my tits and ass while everyone walked by with me yelling for help. They didn't even look or care except to look away or walk faster. But, the part that truly freaked me out was the look on Opar's filthy face when he warned me off Ronicker. A greedy, protective, almost compassionate look from a rapist shit like him. Sick. So much sicker than if he'd just stayed in character. It weirded me out and confused me, which I hated. Absolutely HATED!

Up ahead I watched as Ronicker called a girl named Mel out of line and into his room and shut the door.

A hand pushed my back.

"Think you're cool wearing those fucking gloves? Go you grunge skank!"

I kept walking forward. Past the shut door. My mind doing back flips at everything I'd seen and heard since coming here. Back home in Jacksonville things had been tough, but they'd been the usual kind of tough. This place wasn't tough, it was beyond the edge of reason. By the third day of school I spent most of my time daydreaming about running away to my aunt's house. Then came yesterday, when that shit went down in the hallway. When I'd told the ladies in the office about being mauled in the hall shortly after it happened in a yelling, full on fit, they sent me in to see the principal. He listened to it all, then mumbled some stuff about me making up lies and exaggerating to get attention and how that wouldn't work here in his school. Then he suggested I may have brought on some of these 'empty threats' by flaunting my alternative sexuality in front of the deeply religious children who attended the school.

"How do they even know about my 'sexuality' unless someone from YOUR! office read my file and told them! And how am I flaunting anything? A little bit of makeup, black eye liner, and blue lip stick isn't a rainbow pinwheel sparkler and an 'I EAT PIE' T-shirt!"

He'd smiled as if amused by my rant, then looked me up and down.

"You'll get use to Preston soon enough. And you know, if you're that frightened of the small radical element in our student body that may express their issues with your sexual preference in crass ways we can work something out. Perhaps you can work in the office as a student aide. You'd be safe as a bug in a rug if they knew you were seeing me every day." "Working." He added the word a long second later.

There on his desk was a picture of him and Ronicker with some other man standing in between them. He'd noticed me looking at the picture, then frowned. I remembered how he sat there, looking at me, thinking. His obvious surprise that I already knew about Ronicker; that I'd already connected the dots between the two of them, or been told. Or taken? I'd stood there and watched his wheels turning. Worrying. Wondering. As my own wheels turned and my own guts did summersaults.

"That'll be all Willow. Your mother needs to have a long talk with you about respect. You may go now."

I'd left his office with a stunned and disgusted look frozen on my face. A look he'd seen and hadn't liked. One of the office ladies pushed a track like pamphlet at me and invited me to church. The 'Townie' Prestonian Church that the commuter kids or their parents weren't allowed to attend. Townies only.

"You're not allowed to do that at school," I had told her.

She'd taken an offended step back, looking at me as if I'd hissed like a stepped on snake.

"God will get your attention and it won't be nice," she'd threatened.

The other woman had apologized for her. She told me she was sorry that word got out about my 'condition'. Then she'd given me a sad look, darted a fearful glance toward the principal's door and whispered, 'Good luck'.

"If I had any of that, do you think I'd be here?"

Yesterday was all the proof I needed, and nothing had happened this morning to make me think any different. I was off the edge. Out of bounds. Denial wouldn't do me a lick of good. And pretending it wasn't what it looked like would only make me easy prey. Before I could say 'Don't', I'd be on the other side of something horrible, with a dazed, train wreck expression on my face as I stared back at myself in a mirror, wondering what I could have done different. I knew what I had to do. I had to step up and own this or let it own me. Either let this inbreed shit hole my mother had brought me to eat me alive, or I had to eat it first. At Lakawana Heights with all its thugs and gangs I'd never been raped. I'd been lucky, and careful, but there were sane adults and safe places and people who helped me. And joining the LBGT group had helped too, because it stepped up 'unwanted flirting' to hate crime status, according to the sue happy lawyers that made the rules in Florida. That trick wouldn't help here. This place was insane. If I were going to survive I had to go beyond the edge, too. All the way. No holding back. I had to go there because I was a pretty, little girl who only weighed ninety three pounds soaking wet and every overall wearing male in this school wanted to be the first to eat me alive. I'd seen it on their faces, and not just Larry and his crew. Most of the other townie boys and male teachers eyed me the same way the principal had. If Larry and his thugs got me it wouldn't stop there. They all knew my mother was a drunk who only wanted me because I cooked the food she ate and cleaned the toilet she shat that food into three to six hours later. No older brothers, no father. There was no help for me except the kind I made for myself, and the kind I had in my bag.

An idea hit me as we got to the double doors leading to the auditorium. I left the stream of traffic and slipped into a bathroom, but didn't bother with the already full stalls. I'd been in this bathroom once and remembered the vents for heating were right down on the floor by the sinks, which I guess made sense as heat rises but it sure looked trashy.

Two red headed, townie girls, who looked like sisters, were crying by the sink and fixing each others faces as I pried back the aluminum cover and slipped inside the dusty air duct, pulling the thing closed behind me. I don't even think they noticed me, but it wouldn't matter if they had. Who could they tell? And why? They clearly had problems of their own.

I crawled down the shaft, going from one tiny pool of slatted light to the next. I made one left turn going down the hall that ran past the classrooms on the right hand side. I didn't need to guess which room I wanted. I heard them both. Her crying quietly.

Him doing what he was doing. He was doing it right there on a desk, holding both her hands behind her back with one hand while the other he had fisted in her hair. Both of their pants were down on the floor around one pant leg. It had a familiar, practiced look to it that gave me the chills. I guess they did it that way so they could get them back up in a hurry if someone started banging on the door. The classroom vents were smaller than the one in the bathroom, but they were still big enough to get in and out of. These vents had bolts on this side holding them in place, not the other side. I guess it was done that way to keep the kids from getting out, not in. I undid the bolts on the vent, and I didn't have to worry over being quiet. I pushed the vent out a crack and slipped my phone out the top and video taped it. The phone I wasn't suppose to have according to school rules.

Mel lifted her head and looked right at me, as if she knew I was there.

I watched her and she watched me. It was horrible. I'd never seen anything so horrible and ugly. Mean. Wicked. Dirty. More and more words.. I ran out of words long before it ended. I felt like her. Our eyes connected. My heart in my throat. I felt like it was me just by watching it. My hair. My arm pinned behind my back. My body hurt in that way. Watching him do that. Seeing her face. Her eyes boring into me the whole time. His red face behind her, teeth gritted in a snarl as he did what he did. Both faces looked in pain, as if this were hurting him too. Only he wanted it and she didn't.

"Now, you go tell your brother and see what good it does you Miss Oper. I know he don't like having his sister sanctified by anyone but his daddy, but he'll just have to get use to the idea, and so will you. Either that or have your father call me and we'll work out some other arrangements for you." He laughed as he zipped up his pants then left the room. After getting herself back together she left too, quickly, as if she were more embarrassed to have had me see what happened than she'd have been if I hadn't seen.

I undid the rest of the bolts on the vent, but didn't push it out. On the way back to the bathroom I undid the bolts on another classroom, too. Before crawling back through the dusty vent shaft to the bathroom and class, I went online on my phone and emailed the video to the Pennsylvania Department for Abused and Exploited Children along with a plea for help. I knew that if I went and showed Principal Devry, he'd just take my phone and delete the video and who knew what else after that.

I was jittery and on edge after I came out, jumping and snapping at every little thing. Two commuter girls and three commuter boys actually came up to me during first and second hours warning me to go home. To act sick or call my mom to come get me. Two, cold eyed townie girls told me to move away, out of Preston County. That I didn't belong there. The whole class quieted and watched as I told both groups to leave me be. That my drunk Momma wouldn't move away from a free house and that I was stuck here. And that even if I told the office they weren't gonna do anything. And if I did go home today pretending I was 'sick', what would I do the next day, and the day after that?

"You gonna fight'em off for me?!" I asked one commuter boy angrily.

He backed away, looking sick. Resigned looks passed over the faces of others and they turned back to their own business. For the rest of the day I got dead eyed looks like I was already gone. The commuter girls avoided getting near me as if I might be contagious in a way that had nothing to do with me kissing them, and oddly, the town girls almost seemed to accept me more. The looks they gave me were sympathetic, but a kind of shared sympathy I wanted no part of. That kind of sympathy sent chills up my spine.

That last bit of new kid protection I'd had was gone. I could feel it. So did everyone else.

Sure enough, Larry and his boys stayed at the door of the classroom after fourth hour. Fat Mr. Grant insisted on being the first out the door as we left for lunch a minute before the bell, which left the classroom in the hands of the animals. The three of them practically pushed the other kids on through in their hurry to clear the room as they looked back at me, smiling, ready. I slipped to the back of the class and ducked down and hit the vent I'd loosened up. By the time they'd ran to the back of the class I was in and crawling like crazy. They followed.

Two minutes later I pushed out the other vent and crawled into the devil's classroom.

Mr. Ronicker shot to his feet where he sat behind his desk, his bag lunch spread out in front of him.

"What the hell!"

I looked right at him, practically shaking with fear, and froze…

'Hush him! Finger to lips!' I heard my own voice in my head, ordering myself to action.

Obediently, I raised a finger over my lips, then pointed down to the open vent. I dashed back out of the way as the other boys came tumbling out, already grabbing for my feet. At first they didn't even notice Ronicker. All they could see was me as I stepped backward, but he was there behind the three of them, stepping quietly around his desk and stalking closer. Clay pulled some hand ties out of his pocket and licked his lips. My eyes locked in on the clear plastic things. It looked like something you'd use to tie up a garbage bag. When my back hit the wall I pulled my hand out of my bag. I was already holding the gun. I'd found it in a ditch on the way home from the corner store one day. I knew I had four bullets in the gun, and there were four of them. I couldn't afford to miss.

"Holy shit!" Clay's eyes got big as golf balls as he stared at the gun. They all froze and put their hands up as if I were a cop. Behind them Mr. Ronicker froze, too. I aimed at him first, which made them all turn to look.

"Wait a minute young lady! I wasn't about to let these boys hurt you!" he lied. "And I can't believe you brought a gun onto this campus!"

All I could see as I looked at him was his red face, him gritting his teeth as he did that to me. I'd been watching it happen to Mel, but it still felt like me. If I lived a thousand years, I'd never get what I'd seen out of my head. He'd put that bit of himself into me by force, and now I had something I wanted to put into him the same way. The gun jumped in my hands and the bang echoed inside the room loudly. He dropped right there where he stood. The boys stood there, looking down at him, mouths hanging open in disbelief and not even seeing me as I aimed again. Carefully, very carefully, I aimed in the upper middle of Clay's back. Not too high so I'd miss his heart. Clay didn't drop when I pulled the trigger, he went flying, plowing into Mitchel and Larry and knocking them to the ground like bowling pins. As they tried to get Clay off I aimed again. I pulled the trigger just as Larry was about to shout something. I didn't think I'd hit him at first, but then he dropped and started thrashing about on the floor with blood pouring out the back of his head. Mitchel grabbed a desk and turned it on its side like a shield but it was too small to hide behind and too awkward to move. His arms and legs were exposed, but I couldn't risk missing or even just winging him. I only had one bullet left. Sirens started going off out in the hallway. People screaming and running.

"I'm done Mitchel. I ain't gonna kill you. I'm done." I made myself sound scared. "I just had to stop Larry."

"Don't shoot me Willow, please! You don't understand. Please, let me explain!"

I was ready when he peeked up over the edge. I pulled the trigger and the bullet went right into his forehead. A neat, round hole.

More kids were yelling out in the hallway and the alarm was still blaring. No one had opened the door yet, but I knew it wouldn't be long before someone got brave enough to take a peek. I looked down, avoiding the blood pooling in different places and ignoring the weird way my heart was beating as I stepped over to Clay and picked up the plastic ties he'd dropped. I stuffed the ties in my pocket then tip toed to Larry who was twitching on the floor as he looked up at me. I pressed the gun into his hand and he grabbed it like he wanted it. He was looking at me with one eye as he raised the gun and pointed it at me and pulled the trigger. Click. Click. Click. Click. I reached down and pulled off my right glove. I took out my phone and queued up the video and put it in his left hand, while he kept aiming at me with his right and pulling the trigger over and over.

Click. Click. Click. Click.

I reached out and raked my claws down his wrist, marking him before I slipped the glove back on. The gun lowered to the ground, but his finger kept pulling the trigger while in his other hand the horrible sounds of his sister and Mr. Ronicker continued to play. Both noises seemed at home in the blood spattered room as I tip toed past what looked like bits of Larry's brains to the front of the class. I locked the door then carefully went back to the vent. On the way back through the dusty vent I paused at a hole in the ceiling that I'd noticed on my first pass through. I pulled my right glove off, the glove I'd held the gun with, then pushed it through that rat or squirrel chewed hole and crawled back to the other classroom where I'd started, being careful as I went not to leave fingerprints behind with my uncovered hand.

When I crawled out of the vent to my fourth hour class the alarm was still sounding. The room was empty and the hall outside sounded empty of students, but I knew the police would be here soon. They had to be! I dashed over to the one mirror in the classroom near the back that the girls used to primp with. My white makeup was mostly all gone and sweated off but I brushed the dust out of my hair, off my pants and clothes and cleaned up my one glove, getting the soot off. But when I was cleaning my white top my heart dropped like a rock. Microscopic specks of blood dotted it here and there. They might miss it, but I doubted it. Having one glove gone would be weird enough, I couldn't get rid of the top, too.

OK! What to do? What to do?.....

"Easy, I need more blood."

I balled my hand into a fist and punched myself right in the face, again and again. I stopped when blood began dribbling down my face from my nose. My eyes felt puffy, but I didn't look at myself in the mirror. I didn't want to see what I'd done. I was dizzy, but I didn't hurt anywhere but my nose and there was a tightness of skin in places that were already swelling. I sank down there by the wall. I took the little plastic ties out of my bag then fumbled open my pants buttons and pulled off my own pants. I'd already bled on them pretty good so I threw them across the room. Then my underwear. My bra caught on the ceiling fan, swirling around and around like it had a life of its own. I kept the shirt with me. Warm blood dribbled down my chest as I picked up the plastic ties and put one around my ankles and pulled it tight, until it hurt. I did my hands and used my teeth to pull that one tight, too.

I sat there on the cold, hard floor. I was done. I'd raped the rapists. I'd out monstered the monsters. I'd stared the devil in the eye and ripped his head off and shat down the gory hole of his throat as easy as momma on the toilet doing her business. None of it felt real, and maybe it wasn't. Maybe I wasn't even real. How could this place even exist, and how could I do what I'd just done? It was beyond the edge. Past sanity. And I guess I was too now. I mopped some blood off my bare chest with the shirt, painting myself red before wadding it up in a ball. I used it like a pillow for my head as I stretched out on the floor.

Maybe Momma was right to come back home.

Back to Preston Pennsylvania.

Back beyond the edge.

Welcome Home

The lady cop beside my hospital bed had a nice voice, but cold eyes. It felt like she was trying to look inside my head.

"I know you've been through a lot, but we have to ask some questions. Your mother said we had her permission to speak to you. We've been trying to piece together what happened and we need your help."

"I want my phone. They took my phone."

I sounded nasally through the tape over my busted nose.

"The phone you weren't supposed to have?"

I nodded, giving her a challenging look. "Good thing I did have it, huh?" I made the 'huh' a question. One she ignored.

"Willow, the video of Mr. Ronicker and Mel. Were you hiding in the vent when you shot it?"

I spun my story, leaving parts blank for her to fill in. I said I'd ran into the bathroom that morning to hide from the boys who tried to grab me before assembly, and that I'd shot the video as I hid in the vent. I even said I had the idea of loosening the other vent in fourth hour so I could get away if they came after me during lunch, but that they'd caught me as I tried to get into the vent after fourth hour. While the others tied me up I said that Luke grabbed my phone so I couldn't call 911, and that the video of his sister was there on the screen. I'd said that the gun wasn't mine. The gun was the big, ugly hole in my story, but not that ugly. Even an idiot could understand why I'd brought a gun to school, but I also knew they weren't about to run me up on charges for it after what happened. Still, I didn't own up to it.

I got a nurse to bring me a local newspaper. It called the shootings a tragic example of irony. To be in the midst of abusing a young girl only to find out - at exactly that moment - that your sister had been raped by a teacher earlier that day. They said

---

Larry'd become so enraged that he and his crew went to kill that man for what he'd done, only he'd been so disgusted with himself, and the other boys, that after he killed Ronicker he killed all the other rapists in sight, including himself. The story said he put the gun in his own mouth as he held the phone and watched the video of his sister till he died. In the face of all the horrible facts they still tried to paint a picture of a redeemed young man at the end. It was disgusting.

I watched on the TV in my hospital room as the whole town mourned. Three boys were dead, and a teacher respected by many before this. Four funerals, but hardly a word about why they died or what they'd done. There was sadness and mourning but no outrage. They used words like 'tragedy' and 'heartache' and blamed this and that. If the rapes were mentioned at all it was brief and reluctant.

When I got home from the hospital three days later, my mother was happy. A school lawyer had given her a settlement check for fifty thousand dollars and gotten her to sign a non disclosure agreement. She said they'd already called the paper to stop the story from the reporter who visited me in the hospital. She smiled the whole time, practically dancing around the living room. You'd think me getting raped was the best thing that I'd ever done.

I stood there in the middle of the kitchen glaring at her smile until she wound down and the hopeful grin slid off her face. Something human moved in her eyes for a moment. Guilt. As she broke into yelling instead, I felt a coldness setting in my guts. Goosebumps tingled up and down my arms and opened my eyes wide. Before I came here I'd never 'hated' my mother. Not enough to hurt her. Not enough to kill her. I wished the gun were in my hand. As she yelled I saw the bullet holes punching into her face and fat body in different places. I stood there, looking at her, remembering the blood and the feel of the gun, killing her again and again and again. I stood there and killed her until she shut up and walked away, giving me queer, nervous looks as she went back to her eternal three way orgy, filling her two eye holes with what her TV lover had to offer while shoving whatever bottle she could find into her mouth.

I went up to my room and laid in my bed. I drifted off to sleep counting different ways I could kill my mother like one might count sheep.

Shane Wesley Shelton

On The Bus

The noise and shouting on the bus dropped to a hissing whisper as I stepped onboard. The bus driver looked dead ahead, not offering a 'Hi' or a 'Take a seat' or even a 'Hurry up' mixed with a hopeful leer, which was his usual greeting for me and the other townie girls. As I stepped inside, the other teens gave me sly smirks or sympathetic pained faces as they took in the bruises around my eyes and the tape across my nose, or they did like the driver and stared out the window or at the seat in front of them.

I stood there at the front of the bus looking at them. The sheep and the wolves and the nothings. I hated them equally. The ones who smirked were in their way less disgusting than those who looked at nothing. The ones with sympathetic faces might as well have sneered for all the good they did me or anyone else like me. I'd been here a little over a week, but how much had they seen and heard over the months or years, or been through themselves before I'd ever set foot on this bus?

"Willow, you need to take a seat."

The driver faced dead ahead, but glanced at me guiltily from the corner of his eye.

"Or what?" I asked, dared, scoffed, "What are you gonna do, town man?"

Now his voice was pleading, "Please honey, just take a.."

"Look me in the eye you fat piece of human shit!" I screamed it at the top of my lungs, putting every bit of my outrage into my voice. All of the frustration. All of my hate.

I don't know what happened, but when my vision cleared enough to see again the driver looked pale as a sheet. He didn't look at me, he just swung the doors shut and started driving with me standing in the aisle, panting, red spots still swimming in my vision. Electricity crackled through the enclosed metal space as if my defiant shout had been a lightning strike that had somehow put everyone's hair on end. The vibe inside the bus had changed. Imploded. The sly looks and grins from the

---

townie boys were obliterated. Now they sat there in their seats wearing fear, like the driver. And the townie girls in their long dresses no longer stared down at the floor or at their hands clasped together in their laps like zombies, they had their heads up. They weren't happy or bubbly, but they met my eyes and did not look away like the commuter kids and townie boys.

I sat beside the same nerdish commuter boy I'd sat beside every day. Three stops later the bus stopped to pick up Mel, the girl I'd seen getting raped, the girl whose brother I'd killed. The bus driver didn't look at her either as he opened the door. Out the window I could see a tall man with overalls and a dark expression standing there, watching her as she climbed up the steps. Mel kept her head down as she passed by and took a seat in the back. When the police questioned me I'd asked them when they were going to arrest Mel's father for raping his daughter like Ronicker said on the video. They'd only said that they'd 'look into it'. Obviously they hadn't looked too hard.

Keeping Control

A policeman was waiting for me when I got off the bus, along with principal Devry. They searched my bags right there in front of everyone and the preachy office aide lady walked me to a classroom and had me sit and wait as she sat in front of me and watched. She didn't say a word but her prim, self-righteous happiness was self-evident as she sat there with her holier-than-though look directed at me. She sat there fighting herself to keep her preaching inside as I sat in front of her wondering and worrying why they had me here in this room. And more to the point, what they'd do next.

Out in the hallway I heard raised voices, adults arguing.

"Why wasn't she at the memorial service! She was supposed to be there! Where have you put her!" I heard a woman shout.

"Keep quiet!" the office lady hissed, glaring at me.

Well now I had to shout, so I did. I kept shouting and shouting as the shrew faced woman rushed over. She may have looked thin and frail, but she moved like lightning and it seemed as if she had her hands around my throat before she even touched me, and once she put her hand over my face I couldn't even breathe.

When I came to, a woman I didn't know was leaning over me.

"Willow? Willow, can you hear me?" she asked, face pinched in worry.

"She was having a panic attack and then she just stopped breathing. That's why we wanted her in here." I heard the shrew, her voice scared and perhaps guilty as she lied though her holier-than-thou mouth, to save her own ass.

The woman over me had her phone out. She began talking to the police saying she needed an ambulance.

"You don't need to call the police! She doesn't need an ambulance! You're over reacting! She's fine now!"

"When I came in you had your hands over her mouth!"

"I didn't do anything to the girl! She had a panic attack!" she lied desperately as I stared up into her eyes from the floor where I lay, still panting and fighting off the shakes. I listened to her voice. She lied like a person who needed to convince herself she was telling the truth so she'd be able to sleep at night. It was there, in her face. In her eyes. It made me wonder how many things she'd had to convince herself of in spite of herself. She was bat shit crazy. They argued for a while as I lay there, feeling my bangs and bruises and the panic of my oxygen starved body as it recovered. She kept lying and lying until the principal came rushing in with the school nurse and backed her up. Apparently the police had called him and he'd assured them that an ambulance was not needed. Nice that he was psychic enough to be able to know that without seeing me first.

"You son of a bitch!"

"Hey now!" Devry raised a finger, as if 'NOW' she'd crossed a line.

"You had no right to tell them not to send an ambulance that I called for! You just don't want those reporters to see flashing lights pulling up to your precious school for this girl Mrs. Swartz just about killed trying to keep quiet!"

"She was having a panic attack!" the office lady, Mrs. Swartz, now sounded as if she were about to have a panic attack of her own.

The evil eyed nurse squeezed my wrist hard as she checked me over until I cried out and told her to get her damned hands off me. The lady from social services, Mrs. Collier, chased her, Principal Devry and Mrs. Swartz out of the little room we were in and shut the door hard, making it just her and I.

"This place is insane!" she said with feeling as she dropped into the chair beside me as if she were exhausted.

"Are you okay?"

"Gang raped and strangled." I glared at her furiously, rubbing at the newest of my bruises from the bitch nurse. "Do you always ask such stupid questions?" I spat into a napkin I had in my hand trying to get the taste of whatever lotion that preachy bitch had all over her hands out of my mouth. I was so mad it was hard to sit still. I had a new top of the list. Worse than the rapists, and those who just looked the other way, or the ones who rationalized or made excuses, worse than all of them was this Swartz woman. A religious psycho hypocrite!

"That lying bitch almost killed me! And then she lied about it! SHE LIED!"

"Calm down Willow. Now tell me what happened from the beginning, start from when you got to school, not the assault on Friday."

"You mean start with today's assault." I glared at her. She was already trying to water down what just happened.

"Maybe she just panicked Willow, when you had your attack."

I gaped at her in disbelief. It was starting already. Her soothing voice was such bullshit.

"I didn't have a panic attack! You're just as bad as she is, already lying to yourself and trying to convince yourself that you didn't just see exactly what you saw. You're sitting there trying to tell yourself that this place can't be that crazy." I was breathing hard, furious to the point of freaking out. "Your just like she is!"

"And how is that Willow? How am I?"

Now her voice was sad. Sympathetic. She eyed me as if I were sick. Deranged. The one who had issues and not the other way around.

"Willow, you need to calm down. You don't want to have another attack."

Another attack? And just like that, I saw it. She'd flipped. Now she believed them. Seeing it actually helped me calm down. She watched me, studying me as I studied her.

"You have every right to be angry Willow."

I didn't start at today on the bus, I started at the beginning and I told her all of it. About Larry and Mitchel and Clay, and going to the office. I told her about Principal Devry and his offer to keep me safe if I let him have me. I told her about Mrs. Swartz and her

---

preachy threat that God would 'Get my attention' and that it 'Wouldn't be nice'. I told her about the next day when I saw Mel pulled out of the line of students by that scum bag Roniker and some other girl who was hauled into a class by Mr. White. And I told her again about what happened this morning, about the way they met me there as I got off the bus and took me to the room we were in and how Mrs. Swartz tried to suffocate me to death to shut me up when I heard her out in the hall and started shouting.

I told her the truth, but saw it on her face. "And you're not gonna do shit about it."

With a very tight voice she asked, "Who was the other girl that got taken into a classroom? Who was she Willow?"

The way she said it made it clear it was a challenge. Prove this and then and only then she'd 'maybe' listen to the rest. It was days ago and I hadn't gotten a good look even then. I didn't know who he'd grabbed.

"A horrible thing happened to you Willow. I'm not denying that, but I think you're letting what you saw and what happened with those boys make you see everyone and everything as a threat. And what happened just now with that office aide was way out of line and it will go into my report as a serious breach and a possible assault, but you're going to have to move past it. And I know you feel trapped here, but please, don't do anything foolish. You're not feeling as if you may hurt yourself are you Willow?"

I laughed, surprising her and myself. And then I laughed again and kept on laughing as all the anger and frustration came out that way. It wasn't funny, and it was. Because I wasn't feeling suicidal, I was feeling homicidal. After I reined it in, I simply refused to talk to her any more. She wasn't worth my breath. When she first stepped into the room and said, 'This place is insane!', she'd been a real person. But now she'd become one of 'them'. Not a sheep. Not a wolf. Not a psycho hypocrite. One of the others. She'd seen it for a moment, but now she was blind and useless and nothing.

She said I'd be seeing a counselor every day. I watched as she wrote 'possibly suicidal' in my file.

"Thanks for that. That'll make a convenient excuse for them when they kill me."

She looked up in surprise and covered what she'd written with her hand. I'd been so unresponsive she'd forgotten to be careful.

Shane Wesley Shelton

"Willow." She gave me sad eyes.

"You'll feel really bad about writing that when it happens. You'll feel like shit because it will be your fault. Even if it looks suspicious, what you've written will be there in that file. You'll feel like shit for writing it, but I'll still be dead."

She sighed, and stood.

"You know," I said as she was heading out the door, "when a pedophile teacher rapes a student in Florida they bring in a bunch of counselors and interview every student to see if their are more victims. They didn't do that did they?"

Just for a second I saw the light of 'THIS PLACE IS INSANE' flash in her eyes, then they went cold. Hard.

"They searched you this morning because they thought you might bring another gun to school Willow. Don't bring any weapons to school. They will be searching you every day."

"Great. Who knows where I'll keep my weapons? They'll have to be thorough. Will it be a strip search here in this room or will they do it some place even more private. Some place where it won't matter if I scream. Will Mr. Devry do it himself, or will he have Mr. White do it? Maybe Mrs. Shultz can hold me down and they can both do it."

She gave me a an exasperated look and I laughed, my voice mocking as I said, "Oh NO! That's insane! That can't happen here! You're just over reacting Willow!"

They said I was too 'distraught' to begin classes and gave me the rest of the week off. They called my mother to come pick me up, but when she didn't answer the phone after two hours the lady cop from the hospital came to school and drove me home.

"Heard there was some kind of problem at school today. What happened?"

"I had a panic attack."

"Really?" Her eyes looked at me in the rear view.

I looked back, but didn't answer the doubt in her eyes. Why bother?

Night Terrors

I woke in the middle of the night, my heart racing as I fought the covers. I couldn't remember what was happening and I didn't try to. I didn't want to. I got my phone off the charger that Officer Stacy had returned completely drained when she dropped me off today. I went online. I didn't want to look at idiots making YouTube videos and there was no way I wanted to chat with the small circle of what passed for friends from Lakawana High. I didn't even want to check my email, just in case they saw the news and were trying to email me. I didn't want to talk about it.

I knew 'it' didn't actually happen, but it would have, and it felt like it did. A chill went down my spine and I chased the thought of Ronicker away. That wasn't what I was dreaming about. It was dinosaurs. Raptors. yeah. Dino's were after me. Because they were hungry. Just needed food. And I look tasty. That's all.

Mel's face flashed in my head, her eyes staring into mine, fighting against the happy lie I was wishing for.

An unwanted dream remnant I couldn't shake.

She lived close. Three bus stops down the road, little more than a mile away. I wondered what she was doing right now. Was she sleeping? And if she was, was she alone? Was she safe? I googled Larry Opar and got a load of articles about him and the shootings. There, in one of the pictures of the funeral, was Principal Devry and that other man from the photo on his desk. Only this guy was wearing a uniform. He was the sheriff. I sat there in bed and looked at him for a while, thinking about it. It figured someone would have to smooth things over when someone got brave enough to go to the police. But what did this guy get out of the deal. Unless he got the same thing Mr. Ronicker was getting.

They were all friends. Three friends. Just like Larry, Mitchel and Clay had been. This time it wasn't a chill, but a thrill of discovery that prickled goosebumps on my arm. I smiled. I was figuring out my enemy. I needed to, because sooner or later they'd be back for me. Principal Devry had seen me looking at that photo on his desk. Now that Mr. Ronicker was dead and people were talking about what he did to Mel, he was probably even more worried. Freaked even. Flipping out about what I knew and what he didn't want everyone else to know.

Okay, they were friends, and probably raped girls together. But which girls? Mel? Other town girls?

I scanned down through the story and found Larry's address. Just before I Google mapped it, I thought about the phone. The phone the police had given back to me today. I wondered if someone was seeing or watching where I went or who I called or what I texted on it. That's what they did in cop shows.

I Googled lesbian porn for a few minutes for their viewing pleasure, not mine, then turned it off, all the way off. If I couldn't use my phone, I could always use my feet. It wasn't that far.

I came to my senses as I was pulling on my jeans.

What the hell was I doing? It's dark! I might fall in a well or trip on a hoe or get caught by that rapist pig bastard and end up in his basement for the rest of my short life being visited by the sheriff and the principal and who knew how many others.

I dove back under the covers. There was always tomorrow, when Mr. Opar would be at the mine and everyone else would be at school. And tomorrow I'd bring a knife from the kitchen. Not that little me could stab down a giant man like Mel's dad, but if I got trapped I could always use the knife on myself.

I stopped and rolled that thought around in my head a moment. It was the first suicidal thought I'd ever seriously entertained. I couldn't quite believe I'd had it and that it was real. Not flip or for play.

"This place is insane." A chill went through me. A chill that reached to the bone.

I'd still bring the knife.

Liquor Store

Momma was up when I got out of bed at 9. I wondered why untill she said we were out of 'things' and that she needed to go to the store. I made breakfast, which I usually never did. After I set the plate on the TV tray and put it in the living room, I told her I was going back to bed and dashed upstairs, shut and locked my door and started getting myself together for my spying trip to the Opar's place.

I was tying my shoes when someone tried the door.

"Willow, why's your door locked?"

It was my mother.

"I just got raped!" I shouted through the door, heart racing, attitude and mouth on auto pilot. "You're about to leave the house and leave me here all alone! Someone could come in here! Unless that's what you want! Is the mailman going to walk through the front door, or that pedo lovin sheriff, or the man from city hall that winked at you?! You want to make another fifty thousand dollars and dance around in the goddamned living room as they have my funeral?!"

It was quiet. I stood there in the middle of my room breathing hard, waiting.

"I just wanted to thank her for breakfast." said a small voice, one I barely heard.

I walked to the door, my heart hurting and almost hoping. I leaned up against my side of the door.

"Momma?" my voice was soft now too.

"Yes, baby."

I'd asked before. I'd begged until I swore I'd never do it again, but I did it again.

"If you love me, then send me to live with Aunt Fay, or put me up for adoption to someone far away from here. If you love me send me away, please Momma." I started to cry. All through the past three weeks I'd not cried once, but now I was crying and I didn't try and hide it. "Please, Momma! Think about me for once," I sobbed, "do what's best for me before something bad happens again. This place is crazy! Just let me go to Aunt Fay's!"

"I need you with me!" Her voice was hard. Cruel, like she always got when I mentioned Aunt Fay or me leaving. "And don't even think of running away because I'll have Martin, the sheriff, bring you right back!"

I froze.

Martin?

My heart was the only thing moving in the room.

"Willow?"

"Willow?"

"What are you doing in there Willow?" she tried the handle again. "You always do something crazy when you get quiet like this. Open this door!"

Martin? She knew his first name.

There was a huge BANG! The door crashed into my head and I flew backwards and landed hard on the wood floor. The world spun and spun as she cursed, seeing me dressed and my shoes on. She picked me up and carried me down the stairs. Everything was still rolling, up switching to down without warning again and again as she loaded me in the back seat and spun wheels out of the drive. My head hurt so bad I threw up in the back seat. A few minutes later we stopped. She opened the door and dragged me out and made me stand on my own two feet.

"Now let's go!" She pulled me along with her.

We weren't at the hospital like I thought, we were at the liquor store.

I swayed on my feet and squinted my eyes against the bright lights as she pulled me along behind her, one hand clamped hard around my wrist as she pushed a micro sized shopping card down the aisles of Putney's Sprits and Fine Wines with the other. When she stopped to pick up a bottle I bumped into her. The bottle busted on the floor.

"You did that on purpose!"

She spun around and slapped me. The world exploded in a bright flash of color and pain. I knew I was in the middle of the aisle and there was nothing near me to reach out and grab onto, but I tried, hoping for anything to grab onto as I fell. The hard, concrete floor was under me and I didn't want to hit again like I had in my bedroom. I stretched for the aisles on either side with both hands as dozens of bottles began to rain down around me, busting with little 'Pops', spraying red wine and green glass everywhere as I fell and fell and fell..

Monster In The Bed

I opened my eyes to the sound of the news and a familiar 'beep' 'beep' 'beep' of the hospital monitors. Mrs. Collier, the social service worker, was sitting in a chair watching the news on the TV. She had the sound low, but I heard the hard, angry voice of the woman on TV as she glared at the reporter shoving a microphone in her face. She was dressed in black and they were outside, standing by a limo.

"My boy wasn't even in the room as that girl they found! And he wouldn't have killed himself!"

She slammed a car door in the woman's face.

After that the news went on, a different reporter telling with a grave voice that sounded smugly critical, that the sheriff of Preston County was reportedly not making a comment on the case, but that many parents and other government agencies were pushing for the state to intervene and send in outside "non county" counselors and investigators to work with the students to see if there were more victims or additional teachers or other parents involved in the abuse, as sources close to the victims of the tragedy have claimed.

Collier turned back and saw that I was awake.

"I didn't think you'd mind if I told, but the sheriff is furious. He said I was interfering with his investigation. He wanted to arrest me, but I don't think he'll have the chance."

She looked guilty. Ashamed even. "I may have put you in danger, and for that, I'm sorry, but I wasn't thinking straight. How's your head?"

It hurt. Bad. Horribly bad now that she'd mentioned it. I gritted my teeth against the pain. I had questions.

"What happened to you?" I demanded/accused.

She shrugged. "Lots of things kept adding up. How Principal Devry and the ladies in the office kept acting. Mr. White turning white as a sheet and saying he was ill and had to go home when I insisted on seeing him. The sheriff practically dragging me out of the school to get me away from the other kids, saying he wouldn't allow a witch hunt. That ten other girls were absent today. Ten that had been in or attended in the past year, either Mr. Ronicker's or Mr. White's classes. Mr. Devry refused to give me a list of past student aides, but you should have seen his face when I asked." She gave me a look that communicated it pretty well. "Other teens came up to me when they thought no one was looking, telling me there were other girls. The town girls. Prestonian girls."

"What's gonna happen?" I asked.

"Tomorrow this town will be overrun by more police than you can imagine. State police have already set up road blocks to catch people trying to slip away. They're going to the homes of those missing girls before something bad happens. Religious cults like these Prestonians sometimes do crazy things when they know the game's over. But Mel's already in protective custody, so she's safe at least, and they'll probably arrest her father and mother tomorrow like the sheriff should have but didn't, if they haven't already. It's going to be a zoo."

It was already a zoo. Only now everyone knew. And all this with the police needed to happen, but it felt like a hollow victory. Not nearly what I wanted. And someone should have done something to help Mel a long time ago. And I'd just seen that someone on TV.

"Can I borrow your phone?"

She handed me her I-phone and I Googled the town phone book. The home number for Richard L. Opar was easy to find. I held her phone in one hand and used the room phone beside the bed to make my call. I figured she wouldn't answer anything long distance, but maybe she would if she saw it was a call from the hospital.

After four rings someone picked up.

"Who's this?" It was the same voice as what I'd just heard on the television.

"It's Willow Tearney. I know who killed your boy." I said, not caring that Mrs. Collier was there hearing me.

Shane Wesley Shelton

"But maybe you don't wanna know. Maybe you don't.."

"Who?!" she snapped. I heard her panting on the other end of the phone. In and out.

"When Larry and his two thugs caught me they took my gun and my phone, but they stopped what they were doing when they saw I'd recorded Ronicker raping Mel. They saw that I'd emailed the video to someone so Larry called the school office. They thought I was out cold, but I heard Principal Devry tell them to crawl back through the vent so no one would see them pass through the hall and that he'd meet up with them in Mr. Ronicker's room and they'd decide what to do there."

I listened to the breathing for a bit. When she spoke again she sounded suspicious.

"Why you tellin me this DeLaCroix?"

"I saw you on TV. You acted upset," I huffed out a little laugh, though it made my head about split wide open to do it. "I thought that was such a load of shit seeing you act that way, I had to call. You've let Larry and your husband and half this county rape Mel all these years and you didn't do shit for her. You ain't got the guts to do shit now. Devry killed your boy and raped your girl and..."

Mrs. Collier yanked the phone away and slammed it down on the receiver. She stood by my bed looking at me with wild eyes, as if she'd just now realized I was a monster. Blind as a bat one minute and now she saw too much.

"Why did you do that Willow?" her voice was a thin whisper, her eyes wild.

I laid back in my bed, suddenly exhausted. I didn't answer.

"You lied, didn't you? You lied on purpose, to see if you could make Mrs. Opar mad enough to go kill Principal Devry."

I didn't bother to open my eyes. I answered from the dark, pain filled throbbing place inside my head.

"She let her daughter get raped, and Devry's a piece of shit."

"Willow, if Mrs. Opar gets her gun and kills Mr. Devry, you'll be an accessory to murder."

"He deserves to die and she deserves it, too."

"But, you lied to her. You manipulated her Willow."

"So what if I did. I'm an abused, suicidal, panic stricken teenager who's just been raped, traumatized, beaten half to death by her alchey mother, and I'm in the hospital recovering from a concussion. You gave me your phone and sat there and watched me make the call. Does that make me an accessory to murder, or does that make you an accessory to murder?" I opened my eyes and squinted up at her. "They all deserve to die. If I could kill them myself, I would."

"What else have you lied about Willow?" she said, looking at me strangely.

The nurse came in and sent Mrs. Collier out. She gave me something to help me sleep. I drifted off with scene after scene in my head starring an old woman with iron gray hair and a shotgun. Different scenarios played out, with her shooting either Principal Devry, the sheriff, Mr. White, Mr. Opar or other Preston men. Whoever she shot, in whatever order, she always saved the last blast for herself, both barrels nuzzled right under her chin.

Mel wasn't in any of it, because I knew she wasn't there.

She was safe now.

She was safe...

Safe..

Preston Girl

I woke to a man's insistent voice calling my name. When I opened my eyes, he was standing beside my hospital bed. Mustache. Glasses. Gray hair. Suit. My heart eased a bit as I saw I wasn't alone with him. A nicely dressed woman stood from where she'd been sitting in the one chair inside the room.

"You should have let her sleep." she scolded, not gently as she glared at the older man.

He ignored her. "Willow, I'm Ed, this is Gail, we're with the FBI. We have some questions we need to ask you." He loomed over me, already hostile.

"Back off," I croaked. "Get away from me!"

He leaned back a fraction of an inch. "You need to cooperate Willow," He threatened. "We found the glove you hid in the vent. We know you were wearing it when you killed Ronicker and those boys. And we also know that none of them had gunpowder residue on their hands. They didn't fire the gun." He shook his head and scowled, "You planned it all out in advance when you were taping that girl's assault from the vent. You loosened those vents before going back to class until fourth hour rolled around, and you lured your attackers into that room with Ronicker, where you killed them all. Four shots. Four dead bodies. Two heart shots and two head shots. You set evidence to frame Larry Opar, scratched his arm up, then crawled back through those vents to the other classroom. When you noticed the blood from the blow back on your top - that we've already identified as coming form Mitchel Wayne - you tried to cover it over by punching yourself in the face as you looked into the mirror there at the back of the class. Then you took off your own clothes and tied yourself up to make it look like you'd been raped."

He waited for a minute, I guess to see if I'd say anything. Break down into tears. Deny it.

"What really happened that day? The truth!" he glared down at me gritting his teeth.

I stared up into his angry eyes and opened the windows of my soul all the way so he could see how much I didn't give a shit what he wanted. I didn't even care enough to call him an asshole, or to argue that I tried to tell, tried to get help, but that everyone was in on it. No one would help me, but me. My choice was eat, or be eaten. So, I ate.

As I looked up into his angry eyes I realized with a tiny chill, that I was still hungry. I put that into my eyes and pushed it up at him. Into him. Like a bullet from a gun.

He pulled back right away, a surprised expression on his face. He took a good step back from my bedside, but kept talking. He sounded normal enough, though Gail eyed him with worry and me with something akin to wary surprise.

"I know you were put in a terrible situation," Ed said, backtracking on his hostile tone, "and even if you weren't raped, we all know you were the victim, but it's hard to see you as a victim when you did what you did with such forethought and precision. And Mrs. Collier told us about that very manipulative call you made to Mrs. Opar," he tossed out, shifting gears again.

"Is she dead?" I asked, my voice flat, but not disinterested.

The man and the woman shared a look.

"She may die. She was beaten pretty badly by her husband." Gail said, "She's in a room four doors down, but she'll be going away once she's well enough. If she lives."

"Disappointed?" asked Ed, his bushy gray brows raised and mouth puckered into an almost comical pooch lipped scowl. "You wanted her to die, didn't you?"

I didn't answer. I did notice that he was keeping his distance now. Good.

"Willow," Gail cut in again, "when the police pulled up to arrest him Mr. Opar ran through the woods behind his house."

If he ran that way.... and went far enough....

I looked up to find them both watching me. It was there on their faces. The expectation. The stillness.

Shane Wesley Shelton

What they hadn't said..

"I hope he raped her first." I didn't say it cold and mean. I just said it. Just there.

The two blinked, then shared another look, wide eyes and carefully blank expressions regarded me.

"Willow, your Aunt Fay had come to take you away. She was there when Mr. Opar came into the house."

"Fay!" I scowled in pain and sickened confusion as I sat up. "Is she?" I asked, my heart already sinking.

"I'm sorry Willow."

I laid back again, amazed at the total shittiness of life. Just when you thought it couldn't get any shittier, it did. If I didn't have bad luck I wouldn't have any at all.

"So Fay died and Momma's still alive. Figures."

The two shared another queer look between them.

"Willow, do you remember what happened at the liquor store?"

Something in her voice caught at my ear. Gail and Ed were both wearing carefully blank expressions that were purposefully free of anything but wary sympathy.

"I bumped into Momma and she slapped me."

"After that," Ed prompted.

I tried to remember, but it made my head hurt. "I was scared. I knew I was hurt and I didn't want to hit that concrete floor. I couldn't reach the shelves, and then the bottles started falling."

They waited for more, but I didn't have more to give. I guess they could see that because they didn't wait long.

"Your mother slipped and fell. She got cut on some broken glass and bled out before they could get her to the hospital." Gail gave Ed a look that told me plain as day he'd lied. But not about one part.

"She's dead?"

They didn't tell me any more, and they turned off the TV and stole the remote before the doctors chased them out.

Once I'd taken a nap, I slipped out of bed and staggered my way over and turned the TV back on. Closed captions and the news did the rest. They were calling it a generational problem of learned abuse. Something they believe started out years and years ago as part of their religious belief system, like an ugly, early version of polygamist Mormonism, but unlike Joseph Smith and his followers, the Preston settlement's religious elements hadn't proselytized, sought new members, or spread beyond the small group of original settlers and their descendants. The news said that most of the religious elements had gone away or gone underground in the past twenty years, and the abuse had became more a way of life than an active part of their religion. The man on the news said that the emigrants, led by Bishop John Preston, who settled this valley during tough times, most likely got into the habit of intermarrying between families and sharing their daughters with the adults in the community until they were married off. They said that Bishop Preston had 'integrated' this into their belief system to make the practice more palatable. The mothers, he said, put up with it because it was how they were raised and they believed that this was how things were done. The reporters admitted that most of what they had to share was rumors, local legends and hearsay, but that very little factual information was known about the what they called, 'The Prestonian Cult'. The news said that research into the county marriage records showed a closely kept circle between the original two dozen families over the past two hundred years. However, during the past thirty years, despite all theirs efforts to restrict it, the town grew due to a resurgence in mineral wealth and the need for cheep land. It also became accessible to the outside world through modern technology, all of it combining to make their way of life more difficult to keep hidden each year. They mentioned my video as the last pebble that started the landslide, the thing that turned all the rumors into something real and actionable. I saw right there on that fifteen inch screen photos of my own mother and her sister, Aunt Fay, and heard out loud for the first time there on the news what I already knew must have been my family history. That they had been a part of that world and all its abuse until they'd broke with a two hundred year old tradition and run away from Preston.

I lay there and soaked it in. It all made sense. The feel of the place. The sickly way that coming back here made Momma turn inside out. She'd drank before, but never the way she did since coming to Preston. The distant look she'd get as we passed this house or that place of business. The looks we got from the men and the older women when we went to the courthouse to file papers to claim the house and land. The sly look from the guy who transferred her license and the familiar way the postman greeted her, and the hungry eyed way they all looked at me. It all made sense now. They'd all had her, and felt they had a right to me. It hadn't all been in my head. It was real.

She'd never told me any of what went on here in Preston. Momma knew what would happen here and she still moved here, with me. And she still refused to let me run away to live with Aunt Fay like she herself had done when she was little. Fay was eight years older, so she'd saved Momma from most of it, but Momma didn't to do the same for me. Her own daughter.

I watched, numb as the news played throughout the day. It was like the bullets I'd fired and the blood I'd spilt had burst a dam letting more hot lead and bloody red come gushing out.

Twenty eight families were said to be 'actively involved', with other keeping the abuse within their own families. I watched as those families crumbled on live TV, cops surrounding homes and carrying out either dead bodies or men in handcuffs and weeping girls. Three of the men had committed murder/suicide, the husband killing the whole families and themselves. On the other side of things, three homes had wives or daughters who killed the husbands or fathers, and in one case, the mother and two brothers as well. I saw on the news that they were all being collected. The Preston Children, they were being called. The boys were being taken off for 'counseling' and not to prison for rape. The daughters who'd been abused were also being taken away from their mothers to some place for counseling and 'help'.

I tried to convince them to send me somewhere else. Send me off for adoption.

I tried. But, I was still beyond the edge, and I was a Preston Girl.

Counseling Sessions

After that wake up assault by Ed and Gail, no other cops came into my room to accuse me of anything. None of the doctors or nurses ever hinted that I may be in trouble. They were still worried about my head and gave me another MRI, then drew blood for tests. When I got back, a new nurse took me to a regular looking office that wasn't regular at all. I didn't look around for the cameras because I could feel them crawling around on my skin. Eyes watching me. A tall, sophisticated lady named Carol came in and asked, very nicely, if I was ready to tell what happened when I arrived in Preston or if I wanted to wait for a while.

"Forever," I returned right away.

"That's fine," she nodded, "I'll leave what happened in that classroom alone. I won't ask about it again. If at any point you wish to talk about what happened there I want you to know that you won't be in trouble for what you might say. Now let's talk about something else."

"Like what?"

"Let's start with your mother."

Easy enough. There wasn't much to tell. I went down the cliched list without emotion. No, I didn't know who my father was. Yes, I'd searched for pictures or clues. No, she'd never said who my father was. No, I'd never heard a word about who it might be from my aunt Fay. No, neither my mother nor my Aunt had ever mentioned that they'd grown up in a pedophilistic, hellhole, hillbilly commune. No, they never spoke about home at all until they found out their mother had died and the lawyer contacted them about the house. No, I'd never visited, spoken to, or seen my grandmother before she died. And that was just to start. For two hours we went round and round, when did my mother start to drink, why, any boyfriends, what schools, moves, jobs, and then she finally got around to asking a question I didn't like.

"You're a very pretty girl Willow. With your mother having that many different boyfriends and you going to that many schools, you must have been put in some difficult situations before coming to Preston. Have you ever had to use violence to defend yourself before?"

"I don't want to talk about it."

"We need to know," she pressed.

"You've got my file from my old schools. Read it." I tossed back at her with a little attitude. I'd gotten into a few scrapes and tight situations and made a nuisance of myself any number of times, but there wasn't anything in my school record I was worried about someone knowing. And the rest wasn't anyone's business but mine.

"No Willow, not what's in the file. I need to hear it from you. And not everything happens at school," she leaned in, giving me her version of demanding eye contact. "You're all alone now Willow. You're a ward of the state, and if you're going to be living with the other Preston girls we need to know how you'll manage if they don't accept you. You're still an outsider in many ways, and on top of that, you're the reason they've lost their homes and families. Not all of them will be happy about that. It was abusive and horrible, but it was still the only home they've ever known."

"If they leave me be, I'll leave them be. Being alone has never bothered me."

She considered that for a moment then approached from a different angle. "What if they do exactly that? Leave you alone. You may find yourself isolated and not a welcome part of the group. How will you cope with not being accepted? Day after day. Alone is different from not fitting in." She reached out and touched my hand.

An image flashed across my vision, a ghost image laid on top of Carol's face. A group of young girls were seated around me at a bench. I was one of the girls. No, not me. I was inside Carol. I felt her unease as one of them said something cruel about another girl, then the ugly tightness of a forced smile on the face we shared. Her fluttery insides felt sick as she laughed along with the others. And then the scene changed. A group of men and women stood around us. All of them wearing suits. Ed and Gail were there, both of them laughing along with some others. I felt the same tight smile stretched onto Carol's face. The same sick fluttery insides. The same fear and need to be accepted.

I snatched my hand away from hers and leapt out of my chair. The floor tilted and my vision speckled with dots as I crumpled. Carol caught me and laid me on the floor and ran out into the hall calling for the doctors.

When the doctors came in they were furious. They'd been looking for me everywhere.

"We told you, you could see her for a few minutes - IN HER ROOM - and you've had her in here doing God knows what for the past two and a half hours!" A man shouted at her as he lifted me up while a nurse cradled my head and helped him guide me onto a waiting gurney. Another doctor, talking in a cold voice that was somehow far worse than the shouting said, "You've done a rotation in the ER, you know how dangerous a concussion is. It's inexcusable behavior, and I'll be reporting you to the AMA. This town and the people in it have abused this girl enough and I'll be damned to hell if I let you people do it now just to satisfy you're twisted curiosity as you wave your badges around." He looked right at her and said, "Your sick."

A pinch in my arm. The hot tingle of medicine slipping into me.

"But, she was doing fine before she tried to stand up!" Carol argued and complained and made excuses that they ignored as they wheeled me out of the room she'd hid me in. As they rolled me away, I passed other girls standing in the halls looking down at me. They were my age, or younger, some were older. They all had on white hospital gowns. My blurred vision saw only smudgy colors where faces would have been. Mumbled words floated above me and around me as the medicine carried me to some place farther away.

One Of Us

They'd kept me away from the other girls for the past two days, keeping a close eye on my recovery with a guard posted right outside my door, but I could walk now without falling over or having up become down unexpectedly, and whoever was in charge of things wanted to keep us together. They were moving all sixty-eight of us today. All of us Preston girls.

When June my new 'counselor' brought in some clothes with the tags still on them from the store I asked her why they hadn't just brought some of my old things from the house. June gave me a weighing look then answered my question.

"Your house burned down. Mr. Opar torched it before he took off in your aunt's car."

June was like that. She answered most of my questions directly. No bull. No padding or fluff. I liked that she didn't see me as too 'fragile' or too young, or in some way undeserving to hear the truth. I liked the truth. I liked her. I liked her a lot.

She reached up and caught a handful of long, black hair and pulled it off her neck as she stretched. She paused half way through her shoulder roll giving me a surprised look. I looked away, embarrassed that I'd gotten caught eyeing her in 'that way'. Embarrassed, and more than a little surprised at myself. I'd only met one other girl who could give me butterflies just by walking into the room, and she hadn't given me the time of day. Which made it safe. Distant. Unattainable.

"You don't have to look away Willow."

"What?" I tried to play it off. "I was just thinking about the house and zoned out for a minute."

She smiled sadly. "You really are a horrible liar when it comes to love, but you're very good when it comes to keeping yourself safe and you may need that soon." She gave me a sobering look. "Some of the other counselors have warned me that a few of the other girls are very angry. You'll need to keep your wits about you, don't get caught in a bad situation alone, and whatever they say, don't antagonize them if you can help it. Hopefully, all the hurt feelings will smooth over after a few weeks away from Preston, when they start to appreciate being removed from that hell of a life they were living."

She took a step closer to me then reached out and trapped my face between her two hands. She gave me a deep look, but it wasn't one that said, 'I'm about to kiss you'. But it was one that said she cared about me.

"Whatever these girls say to you today, or forever, I want you to know that you're my hero Willow Tearney. And if I were ten years younger, I'd have been very tempted to let you kiss me."

"Tempted?"

She shrugged. "I'm straight Willow. Straight girls sometimes kiss gay girls. It doesn't mean the same thing to them, or to me, as it would to you. I've seen it in college, but I've never seen it end well for the gay girl, even when that first kiss was sincere on both sides. Once the straight girls get over their initial infatuation, think through what being with a girl would mean for them long term, get pressure from family or friends for being with a girl, or once they satisfy their curiosity they leave them for some guy." She leaned forward and kissed me on the forehead then pulled back again, looking at me like she was trying to memorize me and keep a piece of me with her forever. "You remember that if another straight girl catches your eye. Be careful with that tender heart of yours killer."

I swallowed at the lump in my throat until I could speak.

"I'll try June."

She spent another five minutes helping me get together before leaving to go help some of her other girls. June had five, but most of the counselors had eight to ten. I sat on my bed and waited with my bags packed and ready to go until I heard the commotion out in the hall. I opened the door, a little surprised to see that the chair where the guard had sat for the past few days was empty. I dragged my bag with me as I stepped out into the hall with all the other girls.

"What is she doing here? She's not one of us," said a girl named Anis that I recognized from school. She didn't sound angry or like she wanted to fight, just honestly confused. Two counselors stood in the hall, watching but keeping silent, anxious and ready to intervene depending on how this played out.

"Tearney's not her real last name. She's a DeLaCroix through and through," an older girl said as she trudged by with her bags. Her words drifted back down the hall reaching me, Anis and the dozen or so who'd stopped to stare at me. "She's one of us, whether we like it or not."

I joined the throng, blending in with the others and pulling my bag behind me. Just another Preston girl.

Listening Ghost

After that one comment in the hospital, I endured a four hour bus ride and three days without having a single word spoken directly to me by another Preston girl. But then, no one had hit me, cussed me to my face or done anything worse than glare and give me a shoulder nudge as they passed by in the hall. Even shut out as I was, I still felt accepted by them. I went to class with them, ate with them, walked with them in line, had my medical check with them, went through the bullshit testing to determine my grade level with them. I slept with three other girls who were in my room. I listened to their whispered words for hours at night, and though I did it for different reasons, I joined in their crying, making a mess of my own pillow until I fell asleep with them. I'd never had sisters or sleep over friends, so having other people my age sleeping in my room was totally new. Even if I was a ghost filling the fourth bed in our room, it was still comforting to have other girls there, other girls that I was connected to in some way. I lay there, listening, wondering which of them I was related to, though with over two hundred years of tight inbreeding I was probably related to all of them. They were all the family I had left. The thought didn't bother me, it comforted me. The thought of being all alone, truly all alone - now that bothered me. More than I liked. More than I'd ever expected it to.

During the day, if I sat at a bench where other girls were working on schoolwork or crafts they wouldn't get up and move like I had contagious cancer. They wouldn't talk to me, but then why would they? They didn't know me. I didn't mind my silent isolation because it let me listen in and not have to share or worry about getting involved in the messes all around me. And there were plenty of those. As a ghost, I could stand by and observe as others girls who were coping better rushed in and comforted someone who was falling to pieces, and I didn't have to worry over scolding little ones or trying to get the handful of silent and battered girls who'd clearly been through hell to start talking again. Since no one was talking to the counselors, doctors or nurses, any emotional help they received came from another Preston girl. But best of all, I didn't have to get into pissing matches with the ones who had attitudes or wanted to rule the roost.

That first day in Pittsburg one of the older girls who was trying to become queen bee and lay down the law as she saw it had been 'removed'. Day two another older girl tried the same thing and she was taken away as well. After that no one went after the job, but that left chaos and panic until all the older Preston girls started to boss around the younger ones because they wouldn't listen to or trust the adults who were suppose to be in charge of us. All the older girls took charge, but no one wore a crown now. At least not openly.

There wasn't a whole lot for anyone to do. We had classes, but only for three hours a day. The rest of the time they let us wander about or do what we wanted in the sprawling, three story facility where they had us, and of course they made us go to counseling. One private session and one group session each day. The group sessions were silent and tight lipped affairs with no participation even amongst the smallest girls. I joined in with the silent wall helping to create a united front with no gaps even though the counselors pushed at me specifically to break ranks. The other girls watched me, surprised and understandably suspicious when I didn't dish up the gory details that I'd had no problem sharing when I was at school. I actually learned more about the Preston girls from listening to the pillow talk at night than anything else. What I heard was ugly, horrible, sick, sad - none of which were strong enough words.

"It must bother you that they don't accept you Willow," my frustrated lady counselor said to me during our private session on day three, giving me a long, sad face that was her version of sympathy. She hadn't made this a question. She'd made it a statement. I hadn't shared much with her and what I had shared was none of the things she wanted to talk about, and that was annoying the hell out of Diane. But, the way she felt at liberty to put words in my mouth was annoying the hell out of me. Since I was unwilling to talk or share, it seemed she'd decided to share and talk for me as if I didn't know my own mind. I saw what she was doing for what it was, which was bullshit, but thinking about her or the other counselors doing the same with the other girls made me sick to my stomach. Instead of raping their bodies it was like raping their souls and pushing shit and problems into them that they didn't have or want in the first place.

I kept my reply civil, but firm.

"Why would it bother me, Diane?" she winced the slightest bit as I used her first name again. On day one when she winced the first time I used it, I'd decided to do so from then on.

"Your mother and aunt are gone. You're all alone Willow. You'll need friends. And everyone wants to be accepted." The way she said that caught my ear and made me sit up. She gave me a look as if to question the words from her lips was to admit my own mental instability. And just like that, I was no longer pissed. Her erroneous supposition into my mental state earned this blind and self-important old woman my sympathy, sympathy and a frown, compliments of an uneasy feeling that I made no attempt to hide. An ugly déjà-vu.

"I accept myself Diane," I said as I studied her, wondering what I was missing.

"You seem to be weighing something out. What are you thinking right now, Willow?"

I raised my brows, mildly surprised at seeing she wasn't utterly without observation skills or intuition.

"Asking someone what they're thinking is an open door that leads to rooms you might not like Diane."

She gave me a smug smile that was meant to be comforting and belittling.

"I want to hear it and don't hold back," she said, leaning forward greedily. She readied her forlorn pad to catch whatever scribbles she felt inspired to jot down.

"This is what I'm thinking," I said, eyeing her dispassionately, my voice not angry but clinical and blunt. "I think I may have time for your lazy analysis as I'm stuck here till they put me some place, but I don't have the patience for it." I turned and faced the mirror on the side wall. "I'd like a different counselor." I directed this to the mirror and whoever was behind it. "A counselor who understands that I have my own thoughts and doesn't try to force her own ideas into my head like forcing water down a dry well hoping to get something started, even if it's just denials and anger. That's a mind fuck and I don't like it. And I want a counselor who can see me as an individual and not part of a group of other girls who all have identical needs and issues. If I have to be here and do this shit I'm hoping it might actually be useful, or at the very least that I might make a friend who's sole goal isn't to mind fuck me."

Diane bristled. "Perhaps you'd prefer to have a therapist that's younger and a little more attractive mind fuck you instead. Like June?" Her obvious dig didn't bother me and she apologized the moment after it was out of her mouth, but the exchange hadn't gone unnoticed. Her phone rang almost immediately. I watched as she tried unsuccessfully to school the frustration off her face as she listened to the call. She watched me watching her as she shot angry, furtive glances toward the mirrored glass, looking ashamed of herself for losing her cool.

"You are an excellent manipulator. You got me to lose my composure and I haven't done that with a patient in twenty years," Diane said dismissively as she put her phone away and started to gather her things. "Your private sessions will have to end early tonight Willow. You may go."

As I started to gather my own things, that sense of deja-vu continued to crawl, one that reminded me of being in a room with another woman. A woman who would hurt me or let me be hurt just to make others happy.

"Mrs. Powell."

Diane paused and looked up, hands still on her digital pad. Maybe it was the expression on my face. Or that I'd used her last name. Or perhaps it was her intuition surfacing again, but she set her junk down right away dropped back into her chair and gave me her full attention.

"What is it Willow?" she asked, truly concerned and not mocking or angry.

I didn't know what to do, or if I was just going crazy myself, but I couldn't shake the feeling that she was there. If I asked her if Agent 'Carol' was in the hidden room watching me, she may just deny it. It would leave me nowhere to go and her holding all the cards.

I frowned. Maybe I was going crazy. Maybe my concussion did more damage than the doctors thought.

"What is it Willow?" Diane was worried now. Watching me.

"You're not a bad person Mrs. Powell, and I don't think you would ever hurt me on purpose."

She studied me for a moment before saying, "But you think someone else may. Someone in authority here?"

I nodded.

Diane glanced to the mirrored window herself. Why? Had she seen me looking at it?

Her cell began to ring.

"Don't answer it."

Now she gave me a knowing look, a frightening gleam in her eye as she looked at me.

"Who do you think it is Willow?"

I deflated. She was just like Mrs. Collier. A thinking human with compassion for a brief shining moment, but now she'd changed into some keyed in bloodhound on a scent.

I grabbed my stuff and left.

Breaking In

After my 5pm private counseling session went weird I wandered the facility, going from room to room, walking, freaked out and trying not to show it. A woman dressed as a nurse followed me, lingering in the doorways of the rooms I entered. They were watching me, but so were the Preston girls. Both groups knew something was wrong. Wrong with me. The eyes of even the younger girls in the room darted from me to the woman in the doorway, concern lines furrowing young brows.

A girl at one of the cafeteria tables, who's name I didn't even know, grabbed a squeeze bottle of catsup and headed toward the nurse. She took off. The girl didn't look back at me or come over to say anything, she just went back to her friends and sat back down.

I grabbed a book from a shelf on the wall and sat down too. I tried to forget about my busted head and whatever was wrong with me as I read, though this was far from the best room to do any reading because of all the distractions. There was talking, eating all around me, and the volume was annoyingly high on three big flat screens across the back side of the room where most of the younger children gathered. They were watching three different shows, and were competing with each other, upping the volume on the show they liked to drown out the others. But the noise and the bustle were welcome distractions right now, and the shitty book I'd grabbed soon pulled my fluttering thoughts away from wondering what the hell was wrong with me.

"DeLaCroix."

I lowered the book I was reading to find six of the older girls standing in front of the table I was at. They were all looking at me expectantly. I glanced behind me, but no one was there, then back to the group.

"Me?" I asked stupidly.

"Yes, you!" The speaker, a dark haired and big boned girl named Viki glared, but the others shot me apologies for her tone from behind her back.

I sat up straight, surprised I was being addressed, and by some of the oldest girls here. Apparently the new 'queen bee' in hiding. In the distance I saw that our keepers had also keyed in. Three of them hovered in the back of the room, watching but not interfering.

"We've a question to ask you."

I nodded, giving my attention back to Viki.

"Why don't you watch TV?"

I blinked in surprise. Okay. I hadn't thought that would be the burning question on the tips of their tongues.

"I never liked watching lots of TV, but even if I did I wouldn't watch the shit they have here."

"Why?" asked a girl named Shila who had long, wavy brown hair and haunted green eyes. She wasn't just pretty, she was stunning. Her beauty made me cringe. I knew that beauty for these girls hadn't been a blessing.

"They're only showing us what they want us to see. They're trying to control how you think."

They looked confused, "But, there's a bunch of channels."

"Twenty two!" piped up a cute, gap toothed blonde boldly, as if that number were impossibly huge. The others nodded gravely, all in firm agreement.

I gave them a sad smile then pointed behind them to where our handlers stood watching. "They are trying to get you thinking how they think you should think instead of letting you see the world as it is and letting you make your own decisions on what it all means. They probably don't want to overwhelm you and think it's best to show you little pieces of how life really is at a time, because you guys have a long way to go before you're up to speed on the way things are outside Preston. But that doesn't change the fact that you're being snowed. Now, do you understand what I just said?"

I paused until I got grim nods of understanding. They'd all sobered up, but Viki was still twisted up over the TV. "They let us change the channel though. And if there were more stations we'd see'em, wouldn't we?"

"In Florida I had a hundred and twenty channels and I had the internet on my phone and computer that gave me access to whatever I wanted, whenever I wanted." I gave them a challenging, but not condescending glare. "Haven't you wondered why they haven't given us internet access? I know the school didn't let the town girls use the computers in the libraries, but they were there. I know you saw them. You know what the internet is, even if you weren't allowed to use it. And haven't you noticed that there's no newspapers laying around and not a single news channel in all of those twenty two channels? They're hiding the truth from us and to me that's the same as telling lies."

I raised my book and started to read again, giving them some time to think. I waited untill I heard them pull out chairs and sit before I lowered the book. I could tell by the looks on their faces that they understood what I was saying.

"What should we do Willow?" asked Viki reluctantly, but sincerely.

"Honestly Viki, there's not a lot we can do for anyone other than ourselves."

"Ourselves?" asked gap tooth, not understanding.

"Each of you. Alone. By yourself. You're going to have to think and decide for yourself what to do." Thinking as individuals was hard for them. I knew from watching them at school, seeing them here, and listening to the girls at night that they tended to think like a group. A family. Which was nice, but I knew that was the past, not their future. "I don't know if they've told you or just hinted at it, but in a few weeks they're probably going to break us up and send most of us off to foster homes."

"But, what about our mothers?" asked Vicki, alarmed.

"For every girl who goes back to her mother I'll bet there'll be five who don't. And some of us don't have mother's to go back to. They'll have to put us somewhere. They can't keep us in a place like this forever."

"I think she's right," said a tall girl whose name I didn't know. "I overheard Mr. Browning talking about it with one of the people he was walking around with yesterday." She had short, black hair that barely reached her shoulders and full lips that stayed pressed into a tight, flat line. I'd seen her with Mel a lot, and I'd seen her watching me a number of times from a distance. I'd kept a careful eye on her in return, worried she might be planning to jump me or kill me. She had a wild look to her that made me wary, and she wasn't rail thin and weak like some of the girls. Or pathetically petite, like me.

I blinked as the girl gave me an odd look, as if I'd spoken out loud.

Viki gave the girl a glare, like she was doing something she wasn't suppose to do.

"What do you think it will be like to be adopted?" asked gap tooth girl, a worried, vacant look on her face that made me want to smile. She seemed like the kind of girl who was mostly action and dealt with disasters as they came. Fun and folly hand in hand, but resilient. But this wasn't fun, and the serious expression on a face that was meant for lighter expressions seemed all the more severe.

"You want the truth?" I asked, giving them a face that said right up front it wasn't going to be a fun answer to give or to hear.

They shared pained looks then nodded again.

"Each of these homes they send us to will have parents who have different rules. They'll treat us differently. Some will be absolutely wonderful and will love us better than our own flesh and blood parents ever did, most will be alright, some will be rough and a bit ugly, but nothing like where you came from. Or I came from." I met their gaze head on. They'd all heard about my mother and how she'd practically killed me when she was drunk and ended up killing herself on busted glass. "But, at least one or two or maybe more of the homes they send us to will be worse than what you just left."

"Worse!" hissed Viki.

"What should we do?!" asked gap tooth, leaning forward, tears already filling her eyes. All six girls fixed their pleading eyes on me, desperate for some hope or way to escape from a hell worse than what they'd left behind.

"Calm down!" I told them with a glance toward the back wall where our keepers were watching. "Odds are it will be one of the younger girls and not you. You know how it is. Younger girls are easier to hurt." They looked sickened, but they nodded again. "If you end up in a home like that, do like I did, and fight." I told them flat out. "But don't fight for no good reason. If you end up in a nice home, good. Be thankful. And if you end up where someone tries to hurt you, you fight back!" I said fiercely. "When they tell you to keep quiet or they'll kill you, keep quiet just long enough to get to a safe place, then TELL EVERYBODY! Just like I did. And if they come after you, kill'em if you have to. But don't ever just lay there and take it again. You don't have to live that way."

The group of them looked troubled, all but a fair skinned, brown headed girl who'd not spoken yet.

"You got the devil in you Willow DeLaCroix." She didn't say it meanly. If anything she made it sound as if it were a compliment.

"Not so much," gap tooth added. "Larry and Mitchel and Clay helped sanctify her before they died."

Sanctify me?

I let out a sad sigh. I'd heard this lie whispered back and forth from the girls in my room at night. A fear. A worry. A sick hope that it was over, but believing it was over meant accepting the horrible truth that it was never truly needed at all. 'Who would sanctify us now?' I'd heard them say. This was part of the lies those men told to get what they wanted. And these poor girls still partly believed it because not believing it was worse.

"Larry, Mitchel and Clay died before they raped me. I've never been with a man and I never plan to be with a man."

The six girls looked dumbstruck.

"Never?" asked gap tooth. She looked as if just saying the word caused her pain.

"She's like a boy that way," said the tall, scary girl. "You've been with a girl though?"

I blushed just a bit, then put on a sheepish smile. "No, but its not from a lack of trying."

"It's a sin for a girl to be with another girl. You'll be damned for it and go to hell if you don't change your ways," said gap tooth, but she didn't make it sound preachy or judgmental.

"I can't help the way I am or the way I think," I said wearily, but not as if I were ashamed of myself. I met their gaze then focused in on gap tooth girl. Unkempt, blonde hair hung around her face, her big gray eyes looked a little startled as she stared back at me, but what kept my attention was her mouth, how it hung open just a bit, and her cute smile. The small gap between her two front teeth wasn't big, but it did make me look. "When I look at a boy or a man I don't see anything I want to hold or touch or kiss. They're just people to me. All hard edges, hairy, and ugly. But, when I see a girl I usually see something I like. When I see you, I see your smile and I like it." She blushed three shades of red as I turned my attention to the ghostly pale, brown haired girl who'd said I had a devil. "And you, so pale and perfect." She didn't blush, she looked confused. I looked at the tall girl next. "And you, you scare me."

"I scare you?" she looked incredulous. "I scare Willow DeLaCroix?" This she said as if I were the one to be feared and not the other way around.

I shrugged. "You're tall and strong. I've got small bones and I'm tiny. It's not hard to hurt me." I reached up and massaged the side of my head. The group of girls seemed to do a double take, seeing me again as I might see myself. "It's not hard to hurt me." I confessed my frailty again.

"I'd never hurt you," tall, scary said, and I could tell she meant it.

I smiled. "I know that now, but I didn't before. When I saw you with Mel talking quiet, I thought you might try and kill me for her."

She paled. "I'd never kill! Ever!"

I met her eyes. "I would."

"Why?" she asked, aghast.

"Because some things are worth killing for."

An awkward silence descended on the table. The six of them sat there studying me, each digesting what I'd said in their own way and from the looks on their faces what I'd shared wasn't going down easily.

"Has anyone caught your fancy here?" asked Shila out of the blue.

I tried to fight the blush I felt creeping into my face.

Viki gave me a shit eating grin, looking from Shila to me.

"Shut up Viki!"

They all laughed and laughed, and I laughed with them. Not small, but BIG. It was the kind of laugh that no one had heard since they'd been taken from their homes. Our laughter died as we noticed that every girl across the cafeteria had stopped what they were doing and turned to look our way. Wide open eyes and hungry expressions regarded us, and me most of all. The smaller children had left their non stop TV gazing and were standing as well, looking my way, too. And there were more doctors and nurses watching now as well, some still rushing into the room from wherever they'd been called away from. Almost a full dozen were scattered across the room and packed into doorways.

"We need to break this up before they take her away," Viki whispered protectively.

Reluctantly, the six got up and left my table.

The Test

I sat there alone for a while before I fled the eyes I felt watching me. I went back to my room and shut the door. Later that evening, before lights out, Viki came into my room with two other girls. The pair stood out because they were twins, and my age. They were the ones I'd seen in the school bathroom the day everything went down. I'd never seen them talk, not in school or since we'd all come here. They had identical, straight red hair, freckles, green hazel eyes and matching white dresses. One, had a busted lip that was still healing, the other a black eye. The twin thing still worked, matching, but with different damage. They watched me for a minute in silence then sat at the one small, square table in our room. The twin closest to me pulled out an old coin that was attached to a chain that hung around her neck. She undid the coin from the clasp that went through a small hole then set it on the table top. I watched as she put both palms flat on the table with her thumbs out and touching and held her fingers straight making a big U with the penny in the middle. I watched as the penny moved an inch all on its own. She slid her hands up an inch following the Penny. I watched her and not the penny for a bit. Studied her face as she concentrated, her efforts making the tendons in her neck stand out. The penny moved again, and again. When they got to the middle of the table her twin took over, but she had a slightly different style that she used to 'pull' the penny closer. She held her hands over it and waved the air over the penny and dragged it closer that way, but she didn't touch it. By the time she'd pulled it off the edge and into her lap, the other three girls in my room had joined us. They were all crowded around the table, all of them looking expectantly at me. Viki stood by the door looking nervous and scared, but not because of these two moving things without touching them. The three girls in my room didn't seem freaked out or surprised either. They stood around, keeping quiet as they watched me and not the coin moving on the table top.

The twin tossed the coin to her sister who put it on the table again, but in front of me this time.

"Do it," Viki ordered harshly as she guarded the door.

What the FUCK? I put that into the look I gave her.

"Try," she said, this time nicer, almost pleading.

"You do it!" I dared angrily.

She returned a look that said I was being needlessly difficult and a drama queen then left the door and took the chair at one of the open sides of the table. One of the silent twins put the coin in front of her. She took a moment to get herself psyched then put her hands flat on the table and made the U and scooted the penny a few inches easily. Easier than the twins.

"All Preston girls can do it," said Harper, the youngest of the girls staying in my room.

"What? Why?!"

They all looked surprised.

"Don't you know?" asked Emily nastily. She was a mean mouthed, strange girl with huge brown eyes that overflowed with compassion as she mauled everyone she spoke to then turned around and cried about it. I'd often wondered what would happen if someone just gave the girl a big hug.

"Know what?" I asked kindly, but not because I felt kind. I felt like being a bitch. And being kind in the face of her nastiness was the quickest way to make her cry.

"I told you she didn't know shit!" Sarah, the oldest in our room hissed at Viki, whose only response was a grimace. "Why are you giving her the test if she has no idea what the hell it is?! She's going to think were all crazy! She's going to tell!"

"She's not going to tell," said Emily, already on the edge of tears.

"Tell me what the hells going on!" I glared around at the bunch of them.

"After you try, and if you can make it move, we'll tell you anything you want to know," Viki said firmly.

They could be messing with me with a trick coin, but I doubted it. Which meant this was real. But if it was, then what the hell was going on and why did they want me to try to do it, too? My skin prickled and my head throbbed and my stomach fluttered. I turned and walked to the door slowly and left the room, taking careful, careful steps down the hall. I felt like I might fall. I didn't want to fall. I didn't know what might happen if I fell. Other Preston girls lining the hall outside their rooms watched me with expectant eyes. Hopeful eyes.

Hoping for what? Expecting what? What the hell did they want from me?!

"Willow, what's wrong?" one of the nurses asked as she rushed up to me.

"Don't touch me!" I snapped at her before she bowled into me and knocked me down. I told her I just needed a place to lie down. Alone. Two nurses eyed the gauntlet of Preston girls that formed down the hall ahead of us, both taking care not to touch me as they, and the Preston girls, watched each careful step I took as I passed by on my way to the infirmary.

Losing It

When I woke up in the infirmary the next morning, they checked my blood pressure, which the nurse said was low, then they took my temp which was high, 99.8. They asked me again and again what had happened or if one of the girls had done something or said something that upset me. My only answer to their probing questions was silence. But, if I seemed a little damaged that was no big deal here, or it shouldn't be. There were girls here that were practically basket cases so why freak out that I wasn't talking or that I'd had a bad night. Or that I had low BP or a fever. Lots of the other girls had bad nights, screaming nights, crying nights, the shakes, even fits.

Nurse Bell, the head nurse, said she wanted me to stay in the infirmary and away from the girls to 'rest', supposedly, until my PB was up and my fever gone. Something about her manner made me think that wasn't true. Or wasn't all true. Brenda came into the room and introduced herself as my new counselor. Just like Nurse Bell, she urged me to take a few days away from the girls to rest. Either she was a poor liar and Nurse Bell was too, or I was getting paranoid. Very paranoid. I felt paranoid, frazzled, twitchy even. But for some reason I also felt that the few days would somehow turn into a few more, and then a few more, and then I'd be moved to where ever they sent the other girls, or I'd be somewhere else altogether - who knew where. And right now the only people on Earth who might wonder or care or even ask were I went to, were all here. Preston girls.

Did I want to go, and where could I go to anyway? After what happened with Aunt Fay, her circle of friends wouldn't want me either. I didn't have anyone. Anywhere. Did I want to run away? Not even an option. As weak as I felt, I could hardly stand let alone run.

Did I want to stay with them? The penny pushing Preston girls?

"I really think you should stay here in the infirmary and rest," Brenda said as if she could read my thoughts off my forehead.

An odd expression on her face made me look at her more closely. I noticed she had an earbud in her ear.

Why the hell would she have an earbud in? Was someone talking to her right now?

A sick feeling hit my still delicate stomach like a punch.

Was Carol on the other end of that thing? Telling her what to do. What to say.

"Are you alright?" Brenda reached out to touch me and I leaned away from her. I pressed a hand to my stomach as I turned to Nurse Bell and gave her a nasty, downright hateful glare.

"You're suppose to be taking care of us girls, not working for Carol! She almost killed me in the hospital before I came here, but I doubt she shared that with you!"

Nurse Bell looked shaken, and angry, but not at me. And frightened, which was all me. She opened her mouth, but didn't seem able to form words, or maybe she didn't know what she was 'allowed' to say.

My new 'counselor' pushed between me and the nurse with a too big smile pressed onto her face, "Willow, my name's Brenda, not Carol. Perhaps that concussion still has you a bit shaken." She was still playing her part, except for her wild eyes which gave her away and gave me a chill.

She was here.

I got out of bed and very slowly walked to the door, opened it and left without looking back. No one stopped me as I passed through the medical wing, but a new man I'd never seen wearing slacks and a sweater, followed behind me as I took each careful step through the halls. When I walked back into the cafeteria the Preston girls stopped what they were about, stood and gathered as I slowly shuffle stepped into the room.

"What did they do to you?" asked a girl named Benjamina as she stared at my face and the hand I still pressed to my stomach.

"They tried to take me away."

"Then why didn't you let'em? You ain't no Preston girl no how," sassed a tall girl with hard gray eyes and high cheek bones. She was rail thin, and had ugly, black bruises around her neck that looked as if they'd been made by a man's hands, but she was also probably the oldest girl in the room now. A good bit older than Viki.

She had to be talking about the 'test'. She knew I'd walked out on it. The other girls were quiet, listening. I could see that they all knew and were waiting to see what I'd say. What I'd do.

"Group Session Time." The call for group session came across the speakers. I glanced at the clock along with others. It wasn't time for group for another thirty minutes.

Tall girl leaned in and whispered into my ear.

"You ain't a Preston Girl till you've passed the test, even if you are a DeLaCroix."

I nodded with her head there close beside mine. A small nod, but it was enough.

"Alright then," she whispered back, sounding mollified. "This afternoon after lunch, in your room."

I nodded again, but I felt as if I were about to fall over. I grabbed onto her arm to keep from ending up on the floor. She put her other arm around me, too.

I tried to stand mostly on my own.

"Don't let them see how weak I am or they'll take me away."

"What'd they do to you?" she hissed quietly as she adjusted her hold to do as I asked.

"They didn't do anything," I whispered back.

She gave me a sad, knowing look. "Fever?"

I nodded.

"You need to be sanctified," she said as she started walking me toward group.

I felt tears in my eyes, but I smiled up at her. She was pretty.

"Then sanctify me," I dared.

She gave me a look that made me laugh and I kept laughing. I laughed all the way to group, drawing concerned looks from the workers and the girls walking with me.

Visions

They broke group up into four circles with twenty or so girls in each of the session rooms, where the chairs were already set in a circle with a counselor in the middle and two helpers hovering around. I'd been with the same group as the girls from my room, but this time I went where I was led and sat where I was seated in the same group as the tall, gray eyed girl who blushed so pretty when I asked her to sanctify me.

The other girls in this group were the oldest of the girls here, and they were also some of the most obviously damaged. One of them was blind, a bandage wrapped around her eyes. Two were in wheel chairs with IV stands holding bags that dripped, dripped, dripped, distractingly. I watched those falling drops as the others got settled, letting the drip, drip, drip hold me. Comfort me.

"Ursa, you brought a guest, how nice. It's good to have you with us Willow."

"Willow?"

I blinked at hearing my name and looked into the middle of the circle, coming awake. The fat woman seated on the swivel chair in the center squinted her eyes as she smiled at me.

"I'm Mrs. Kathy, and I think we all know you, but you may not know all the girls here so lets introduce you around." She went around the room with her overly happy voice giving the name for each girl in the circle. "Melanie Opar." Three from my right she introduced Mel then moved on to the next girl. Mel didn't look at me. She didn't look mad, but I guessed that she must be, since I'd more or less killed off her whole family. On around the room Kathy's happy voice went until she got to the tiny wisp of a girl sitting on my left. "And this is Holly Doutch."

"Now!" she brought her hands together in a clap and scrubbed her palms while she pinned me with an exaggerated smile. It was a move that a teacher over a class of three years olds might pull to get her little charges revved up, or to hold their fragile attention. I watched, my attention captivated, but in that car crash kind of way

---

where you can't pull your eyes from the twisted metal and the bloody gutty mess. A YUCK! expression was frozen onto my face as I stared at Kathy with disbelieving eyes. The other girls around the circle didn't even show disgust or horror. They sat in their chairs and gave her blank face, zombie face, please kill me face with little tremors or twitches added on. After three days with this woman I'd be there to, but for now the horror had me.

Kathy addressed the circle, "I hope you remember what we talked about yesterday and that you've been thinking on your strong emotions because it's time to share. And remember, its okay if that strong emotion is anger, or fear, or sadness, or even joy!" As she named each she mimicked that emotion on her fat face. "And I heard someone laughing as they came in, so someone here in group - I KNOW - has some joy to share!"

She looked at me, "Willow? What where you laughing about?"

I looked around at the other girls, surprised and a bit awed as I realized that every single one of them was pretty. Every one. Viki wasn't in the circle or she'd have blown it. Even the ones in the wheel chairs. Even the blind girl. Every one was beautiful in her own way.

"You can share Willow," urged one of the helpers standing behind my chair like Jiminy Cricket's voice.

As I ignored the voice behind my head, June's voice took it's place, like a different cricket, but one I actually cared to listen to as it warned me not to fall for a straight girl.

"There's no need to be scared." Kathy was practically salivating for me to drop any verbal ripple into what had probably been a silent pond for the past three days.

Regretfully, I went back around the room again, matching the names of these girls with their beautiful faces, but the girls I was appreciating started looking back at me, giving me questioning looks, glares, and Ophilia actually gave me an evil grin. It sent a chill down my spine. Did she know what I was thinking about?

She looked right at me and nodded.

I looked down in my lap, my face burning hot as the rest of me froze. I fought to keep the shakes from taking hold.

"What were you thinking right now Willow? Don't be frightened honey. I know this is a new group of girls, but you can share whatever you like here. You're safe here."

This was crazy. She was crazy,

'Ophillia, I can't help it if I think you're pretty.'

Who was I kidding? I was crazy, too.

I felt dizzy, and hot, and chilled at the same time.

I leaned my head back in my chair and looked straight up, not out at the girls. I started to count and recount ceiling tiles, going in a circle with the four tiles directly overhead. In the waiting quiet of the room the steady drip of the IV bags set the tempo of my counting, helping me drift away from where I was.

Drip.. Six. Drip.. Seven. Drip.. Eight.

"Willow, if you don't share you'll have to go back to your old circle. Just a little bit and you can stay. Tell us what you're feeling. What are you thinking about right now."

Drip.. Eighteen. Drip.. Nineteen.

I lifted my hands up over my head and imagined it raining, cool drops falling onto my hot face and upturned palms.

"Willow, you'll have to go now if you don't have anything to share."

"Water, water, everywhere, and not a drop to drink," I heard myself say sadly.

"Has she got a fever?" asked a voice from across the circle.

"She's makin my skin crawl!" another voice complained angrily.

I looked down to see who'd spoken.

"I think so. She's hot, and she's got the chills," said Ursa from the chair on my right.

"Feel her head Holly," said another girl, concerned furrows marring her otherwise perfect brow.

"Be careful!" someone else warned.

The small girl to my left reached up and pressed her hand to my forehead..

One second I was in my seat in the group session room, and then I was there again, fourth hour at Preston High, my stomach a tight nervous knot as I sat in the back of my own head, watching as Luke, Mitchel and Clay rushed the others out of the class. I felt it all as if it were all happening again just as it had the first time. My heart was racing, but not like a panicked rabbit's. It was fast, but also angry. I was darkly determined as I slipped to the back of the class and dove into the vent. I relived it, that mad dash through the vents, then felt my heart nearly stop when I crawled out and saw Ronicker. I froze as what he'd done to Mel earlier that day flashed in my head all over again.

Something was wrong!

I wasn't moving!

'Shush him! Finger to your lips!' I snarled to myself.

I watched as this 'memory' actually heard my voice and moved, raising our hand and pressing a finger to our lips to hush Ronicker, then pointing to the vent as I waited for the boys to arrive.

Good. We were back on track.

I felt the exact same thrill of girlish terror shoot through our shared body as they tumbled out and almost grabbed my legs. Mitchel's smiling face was there again as he came at me with those plastic ties gripped in his hands. I was in the 'zone'. Oblivious to everything but what had to be done. My utterly remorseless and precise thoughts skimmed by as I pushed hot lead into Ronicker's heart, raping him where he stood, just as he'd raped Mel. I relived the careful, deliberate destruction of Mitchel and Larry. Then Clay and his begging as he hid behind the desk until my gentle, lying words lured him out. In my heart I never once considered letting him live. There was no restraint. No pity. No option. Only death. Only blood.

The world spun, faces flashed by in a muddy blur as I shivered.

Wetness ran down my face and chest and back.

"Wet her hands, too! Not the backs! Turn'em around Vy!"

The girls who could, had left their seats and were crowded around me. One was kneeling in front of my chair. She had my hands by the wrists holding them out to the side as another girl poured water onto my palms from a pitcher. Holly was still in her chair beside me shivering and dripping wet, too. She had her eyes squeezed shut so tight she looked like she never wanted to see again. Never wanted to see whatever it was she'd seen. She pitched forward and retched onto the girl kneeling in front of me.

The nurses came in and claimed me and Holly, but not without a huge fight. In the end we went to the infirmary, but some of the girls went with us, and four of them went with me into my room. I watched, from what felt like outside my own body, as Nurse Bell and doctor Doughtry argued with the older girls, whose claim to me was being supported by Carol and the man in the sweater and slacks who'd been following me earlier. Carol called him Vincent.

"They are use to taking care of their own doctor Doughtry. Just give the girls three hours and if there's been no improvement in her condition by then you can start more traditional treatments," Vincent said.

Ophilia gave the doctor a shove. "Don't think ugly thoughts about me and mine!"

I closed my eyes as they argued back and forth beside my bed, trembling as visions of red splashed before my eyes again. Blood dribbling out the back of Larry's head. I tried not to think about being there again, in that room, of how I got there, of why it happened again, of the blood, of Ronicker's red face.

The arguing stopped and then a sweet sound filled the room. A humming. Humming female voices. When I opened my eyes I saw that Ursa, the red headed twins, and

Ophilia were around my bed, each of them dangling their own coins over me, each coin hanging from a chain as they hummed.

The coins turned on the end of the chains without the girls touching them or twisting the chains. They turned and spun faster and faster flashing in the overhead light. It captured me like the drip, drip, drip of the IV bags and pulled me in. The humming never stopped filling the room, or filling me until that was all there was inside my head. Two girls hummed as the other two drew a breath, back and forth.

I felt light.

Faster, faster, faster they spun.. until there were four flashing balls of light and not four coins.

I wanted to be with the lights. With the sound. A part of both. I began to hum with them. I let myself go and hummed and hummed and hummed, up to the lights. I was one of them, with them, a part of them, a part of the sound, a part of the light.

Inheritance

When I woke in the infirmary I was surprised to find myself alone. I'd always liked being alone before, but I'd gotten use to having other people in my room with me - other girls my age. I lay there weighing out the difference between the background noise of other lives and the silence and stillness that was such an intimate part of being alone, where my own sounds were the only ones to hear, my own thoughts the only ones that mattered. After a few minutes, a nurse came in to check on me. She brought me breakfast. When she came back to take my tray, two men in suits followed her into my room along with Dr. Doughtry, who stayed at the back, by the door, observing silently. One of them looked like a cop or something like one. He had a suit, a well trimmed beard that circled his mouth, and he was fit. He was what most girls would think of as ruggedly handsome. That was just a guess, as I wasn't 'most girls', but whoever he was, he had honest eyes and didn't seem too awful. The other guy looked more like a businessman. A businessman here on business. He had an envelope, a black binder and an old, beaten up box tucked under one arm that looked heavy from the way he held it.

"Willow Tearney?" he asked, as if he didn't know for sure who I was.

"DeLaCroix," I replied without hesitation. I'd been called DeLaCroix more than my own first name for almost a week now. And no one, not even the counselors or nurses called me Tearney anymore.

The man was stunned, but only for an instant. He quickly recovered and moved on with what he'd come to say.

"My name's Todd Goins." He pulled out a business card and set it on the rolling breakfast table that stretched over my bed. "I'm your aunt's attorney. Fay Tearney left behind an inheritance which I'm here to see distributed according to her wishes as set forth in her living will which she last updated," he opened the binder and peeked at what was inside, "seven years, four months ago. The house in Nashville is already under contract and those monies will be added to what she had in savings - minus inheritance taxes. Added to that you'll have the two hundred thousand dollar insurance policy she carried automatically as an executive VP of Cornerstone

Cabinets. We can put this money aside for you and arrange a weekly allowance, but there is one item we need to discuss first," he paused to give me a level, appraising look. "How do you feel this morning Willow? You've been through a lot lately, and if we need to wait on this a few weeks, or even months, we can."

He looked like he'd like that very much.

"No, we can't," I said by reflex, to be difficult and a pain in his ass. And because what I wanted was almost always the opposite of what everyone else wanted.

I made, "Lets get it done," my verbal coup de grace to kill the last of his reluctance.

He made a face that basically said, 'whatever' and stepped aside letting the other man speak.

"Willow, are you sure? There are big decisions that need to be made," he said, sounding concerned. "Are you sure you're able to make decisions about your future or do you need some time to recover?"

"Can you handle the truth?" I asked bluntly.

He cracked a smile that looked genuine. "Yeah, I can take it."

"I'm probably more sane and able to do that now than I will be tomorrow, or the next day."

The two men shared a little concerned eye contact. Together they glanced back to the doctor who shrugged.

"She's probably right," he backed me up, just like that.

"Are you saying her mental state is degenerating? That she's slipping away or in some way impaired?"

Doughtry gave me a tight smile then spoke to the two men. "I will not add to what she said. I'll simply agree with it. And I find her honest assessment as a good sign that she's in her right mind, or as much of one as she'll ever have. She has some unique difficulties, of a nature I'm unable to discuss, that are unique to the Preston

Girls, and she's had a severe concussion that's probably done some permanent damage to her balance if nothing else, and she's aware of both of these problems."

The lawyer nodded like he got it. "So, if she said, 'I'm fine..'" he led, motioning to Doughtery.

"Then you'd have a problem," Dr. Doughtry filled in. "Willow seems quite cogent and able to think clearly this morning. The nurse checked her and she's no longer feverish and her pressure is much better. I suggest you do as she's asked and let her make her decisions concerning her inheritance and her name."

"Does that satisfy the court?" asked my aunt's lawyer a bit smugly.

The other guy nodded, but he didn't seem happy about it.

The lawyer turned back to me and pulled out an envelope from which he took some legal looking papers.

"All you need to do is sign and the money is yours. You'll be given an allowance to live on until your eighteen when the entire sum will be available. But I must say again, the money is for Willow Tearney. not Willow DeLaCroix. You'll have to claim the funds and sign for them as Willow Tearney."

I laid back in the bed, thinking. I knew very little about my family, but I did know that Fay had run away from home when she was sixteen, but came back eight years later when she heard her baby sister had gotten pregnant at 14. She'd put a ladder to the side of our old house in the middle of the night and stole my mother, her little sister, away from Preston. I knew that she changed mother's last name to Tearney, like she'd already done for herself, so when I was born I was a Tearney, too. When I was old enough to wonder why my mother was always so mad at my aunt, she refused to tell me, until one day when she was drunk and angry because I'd asked to go live with Fay. She'd said that Fay had tried to force her into getting an abortion when she ran away, but that she'd refused, and that the only reason I was even alive to argue with her was because she loved me and hated Fay. I'd never believed her. We'd argued about it and I'd called her a goddamned liar to her face, defending my aunt.

A tingle of sick certainty slid down my spine.

My mother had told the truth.

My mother had told the truth, and Fay had lied to me. I'd believed her even though I felt, and knew deep inside, that something was 'off" with Fay's denials. I'd been horrible to mother for making up such a horrible lie that I was afraid might be true. And Fay had let me believe those lies all these years even though she saw what it was doing to us. To me. Thinking back on it, I could see that she'd been too ashamed of the truth, and that she'd cared more for me and my affection and loyalty than for her drunken embarrassment of a sister's. So she'd lied and did what she had to do to keep up that lie. And there was no one else around to ask. And neither of them would have ever told me the truth about this place and how they grew up. Not in a million years. They both did their best to forget Preston in their own ways, Momma with drink and men and Fay with work.

What was a name anyway?

Why did it matter?

"She put that in her will, just that way? That I had to be a Tearney to have anything of hers?"

"Yes," was his short answer.

"Sign the documents Willow, you can still call yourself whatever you want." The other man was upset with the lawyer, or at the situation. "Legally your name is Tearney."

"Not your place to pressure the girl one way or the other. Let her decide," Goins scolded carefully.

The two went quiet, one sullen and the other anxiously waiting, both watching me as I thought it through.

If she wrote it that way then the name mattered to Fay, and mattered a lot. Maybe she thought Momma might do exactly what she'd done and move back to Preston with me and I'd become a DeLaCroix again. In a way, she'd given me and Momma her own name, like we were both her kids. I know she'd had her tubes tied so she couldn't have any children, so it made sense that she'd want me. She'd never married and lived alone. I was the only child she'd ever have. The only one she wanted to include in her private island of a life.

But, I wasn't hers.

And if Momma had told the truth, then she really had tried to kill me.

Even dead as she was, Fay was still trying to keep me from being a DeLaCroix. Trying to put her name on me. Trying to make me her's. If I'd not spent the past week with the Preston Girls, watching how they watched me, listening to how they said my name and seen the respect they showed it, and me because of that name - I wouldn't have given any of this a second thought.

I thought on the girls who'd been staying in my room and how if felt to have them there. To hear their whispers at night. What it might be like to join in with them. Be like them. And then there was yesterday and all the mess I'd caused and how they'd taken care of me. How, even when they were mad or suspicious, they still didn't push me away.

They cared about me and wanted me, or they had so far.

I had a choice. Did I want to be the only Tearney on Earth, a girl with no home or family, but with money of her own? Money she got from a woman who tried to killer her and lied to her all her life. Did I want that, or did I want to be the last DeLaCroix, and a Preston Girl?

Which one was I?

I knew of only one sure way to find out.

"Do you have a coin?"

The lawyer looked annoyed as he started to search his pockets, but the other man quickly produced a coin.

"Will a quarter do?"

It was heavier, but why not? Impossible was impossible. I nodded.

He pulled his hand back before he gave me the coin as if a terrible thought just occurred to him.

"Willow, your not going to flip on this are you? This isn't the kind of choice you should let a coin make for you."

He had kind, caring eyes. I gave him a sad smile. He had no idea how wrong he was.

"I'd like some privacy, and that quarter."

DeLaCroix

Knocking... Knocking on my door.

It opened a crack and Dr. Doughtry poked his head into the room. I returned his gaze with dazed, distant eyes. I blinked, breathed in and out, but said nothing.

"Willow, are you alright?" He rushed to my bedside, face already pinched with worry at the sight of me. He grabbed my wrist and eyed his watch, checking my blood pressure.

"You had another episode didn't you." It wasn't a question and I didn't bother to answer.

"Is she alright?" asked Fay's lawyer.

"What happened!" demanded the other man who'd never named himself.

"Your blood pressure's up again," Doughtry felt my head, "and the fever's back. Should I have them bring the girls to see to you or give you something myself Willow?" He let out a frustrated sigh.

"Get them," I said numbly.

He nodded, then walked to the door and called for a nurse, but didn't leave the doorway. He stood there, keeping me in sight and keeping an eye on my other guests as they crept closer to my bed.

"I can come back, too.."

"DeLaCroix," I said firmly, surprising both men.

My unwanted advocate stepped forward, "Willow, please just sign the papers!" he begged. "That money will help you have a good start in life and if you don't take it, it'll just go to UNICEF! Just sign the damn papers!"

The fog parted as I found my anger.

"I don't want Fay's damn money! I killed her! And I'm glad she's dead!" I hissed viciously.

"I know you feel guilty because of the call you made that sent Mr. Opar on a rampage, but you couldn't know this would happen, and you don't have to feel guilty about taking the money. And anything Fay may have done back then she clearly didn't feel that way now! She went to Preston to save you, Willow! Please don't do this!" he begged.

"You'll both have to go now." Dr. Doughtry took charge of the room and pushed in between me and my court appointed advocate, if that was what he was, but the lawyer wasn't done yet.

"Willow, do you claim the name Tearney or DeLaCroix?" he asked from behind the broad backs of Dr. Doughtry and the other man.

A flash of color pulled my gaze to the doorway where Ophilia and Ursa stood, listening.

I met their gaze as I said, "DeLaCroix." For them I added, "I am a Preston Girl."

"Does this satisfy the court?" asked the lawyer.

"You're a son of a bitch," the other man growled in reply.

"No, that would be my client. I'm only serving her last will and testament, and if that will is to be a bitch from beyond the grave - then so be it. Considering the situation it almost seems justified."

Doughtry turned on the man. "Be civil."

Goins ignored the doctor's glare and took the papers and handed them to the other man instead of me. He stomped across the room to a dresser and quickly signed in a few places then handed the papers back to the lawyer. He looked spent and sick at heart. He didn't even look at me as he finished his business with my aunts attorney and in just a minute he was through the door and gone.

Shane Wesley Shelton

"Whether you know it or not, and whether your aunt intended it or not, you've still done a good thing here Willow. The money won't be wasted. The proceeds of the house, the personal items and all the rest of your aunt's money as well as the insurance payout will be given as a charitable gift to help underprivileged children. But, your Aunt also left a letter and the contents of this box to a 'Willow DeLaCroix', if such a girl was found to exist," he said as he looked at me. "And as she most certainly does, I shall need to have you sign for these items with that name."

Dr. Doughtry got out of his way as he set a piece of paper on the bedside table and rolled it into place then handed me a pen. I had to ask the lawyer how I was supposed to spell my own last name because I didn't know for sure.

'DeLaCroix', no spaces, three capitols

"It's French. It means, 'Of The Cross.' Which may seem strange, but it's actually not that uncommon of a name," He said as he set the beat up box on the table and set a key beside the box. He eyed the box with grim curiosity and a little trepidation. "The French like religious names.'" He said distractedly as he placed a faded letter on top of the box that had no writing on it to indicate what it held, or even who it was for.

"Willow, I hope with all my heart that whatever's inside this box is worth more to you than what you just let go. And I want you to know, I do wish you the best. Please don't be upset with me for carrying out your aunt's wishes. I'm just the messenger."

I looked at the man, guessing by his expression that he felt I might be able to do something unnatural, like curse him or cast some black magic his way. I didn't particularly care for the man, but as he said, he'd been the messenger. I figured I'd let him make is own peace, if he deserved it.

"Did you look in the box?"

"No," he said right away.

"Then you will live."

He pursed his lips and thought on that for a moment, then nodded, looking relieved.

"Would you like us all to give you some privacy Willow?" asked Dr. Doughtry as he eyed me and the box with equal concern. He didn't think me being alone was a good idea, and being alone with whatever was in that box he liked, even less.

Mr. Goins was the first to go, saying a final farewell and casting a final, fearful look toward the old box before slipping out the door.

I looked at Ophilia, wondering if she really could hear my thoughts.

'Stay', I thought to her.

"She wants us to stay."

Dr. Doughtry looked hesitant. "How do you know?"

"Because she's one of us. She always has been." Ophilia said, giving a confirming glance to Ursa.

Vincent appeared in the doorway looking as if he very much wanted to see me and to see what was inside the box. Ophilia gave Doughtry a glare that said he was an idiot and Ursa shooed him out of the room and slammed the door on him, Vincent, and the other curious faces that had sprung up out in the hall, all peering into my room.

"Did you really mean to kill your aunt when you called the Opars?" asked Ursa the moment we were alone, as if she'd barely been able to hold back the question that long. "Holly told us what you did to Larry, Mitchel, Clay, and Mr. Ronicker." She eyed me with fear, loathing, and something that looked like pride.

I gave her a deadpan look, then frowned, but not at her. "I actually meant to kill my mother or Principal Devry when I called over there, but then Fay'd stolen my affection by lying to me all these years and she did everything she could to put her own name on me, so I guess I got what I wanted after all. And there's still time to kill Devry if he's not already dead."

They both stood there looking troubled.

I sighed. Explanations were in order it seemed.

"Back when Fay stole my mother away from Preston she was already pregnant with me. Fay tried to force her to have an abortion, and when my mother told me what Fay'd done she lied about it. And she was ugly about it. Trust me," I met their reluctant expressions without flinching, "she had it coming."

"Have you killed any other people?" asked Ophilia.

Garvey. Momma's old boyfriend's grinning face flashed in my head.

"Who was he?" asked Ophilia, a distant look on her face.

"One of Momma's boyfriends, who tried to sell me one night to one of his druggie friends he owed some money."

"Did the other man.."

"What? Sanctify me?!" I glared.

Ophilia and Ursa both looked away, unable to meet my outraged glare with the faces they hadn't realized had filled with hope.

"He got a hell of a lot closer to it than anyone else ever had, but no, he didn't. I told him he might as well kill me if he did because I'd be down at the police station telling. So he did things that didn't leave marks or DNA until I'd scratched him up enough to make him worry about what I might say, then he went out and grabbed my mother and took her into the back room instead and got his payback out of her. I'm still a virgin if that's what you're asking. All my sin is still my own."

Ursa was looking from me to Ophilia, frustrated and trying to keep up. "You killed the man who sold you, but what about that one that got on you and your mother?"

I smiled at the happy memory. Smiled at the quirks of fate that happened so often with people I wanted to kill or hurt.

"He's probably being sanctified daily." They gave me sick, blank look, not understanding the hint so I spelled it out in much greater detail. "He's in jail for slitting Garvey's throat and raping my mother. I took the knife from his pants he

---

left in the hall and slipped on his jacket and shoes then snuck up on Garvey while he was sitting on the couch watching TV. He was so drunk he barely realized what was happening until I was to the other side of his throat." I remembered the blood had been so warm as it gushed out onto my hands. Ophelia rubbed her hands on her dress, that distant look on her face again as I continued. "I tromped around in the blood in his shoes then used the jacket to wipe the fingerprints off the knife. I left the knife, the shoes and the jacket by his pants outside Momma's bedroom and went and called 911."

"You're a murderer Willow DeLaCroix," said Ursa, not making it an accusation so much as a statement of fact.

I nodded. "But that's not all I am." I reached down beside me in the bed and pulled out the quarter, though it didn't look like a quarter anymore. When I'd tried to make it move I'd focused my gaze on it, then closed my eyes, keeping the image of the quarter in my head. Before I moved it I first tried to get my hand around it with my mind and pick it up, or at least get a feel of it before I tried to shove it. I'd strained so hard my tightly shut eyes went red and my whole body ached with the strain of what I'd been trying to do. When I finally felt like I'd gotten ahold of the thing and opened my eyes and saw what I'd done I'd fainted for bit. When I woke I saw that the quarter hadn't budged an inch. It sat in the exact same spot on my stomach there in the bed, crushed in from all sides as if squeezed by a giant's hand.

"Willow." Ophilia looked up from the coin, sympathy in her eyes and voice. "Holly told us that you don't know why we let the men have us the way we do. That your Momma never told you what happened to the first of us, and why we put up with living this way. There is a reason for it."

"Not now," Ursa said, glancing at the door. "We'll tell her later. Right now we got something else we need to deal with." She looked to the box and the letter. She picked up the old key and handed it to me. "They won't stay out there much longer. Open it."

Ophilia slid the box to me and nodded her grim encouragement.

"Whatever's inside, we'll deal with it together, Preston Girl," Ursa said when I hesitated.

Shane Wesley Shelton

I put the key in the lock, turned it and pushed back the lid. The two girls leaning in on either side of my bed hissed like snakes and backed away.

"What it is?" I asked, not understanding their alarm. It looked like a weird, old charm. Four, ugly nails were strung together onto a leather cord.

The door opened without a knock.

"Willow, may we.."

The three of us looked to the opening door, feeling the same thing, wanting the same thing. The door slammed shut so hard it buckled, black cracks reached out like spider legs toward the top and bottom corners of the frame.

Ophilia and Ursa shared a look over me and the box then sprang into action. Ursa grabbed a box of kleenex and pulled out a dozen sheets she used to lift and wrap the bracelet while Ophilia opened the letter and quickly held it in front of me, leaning in and reading it along with me as frantic voices called to us from outside the stuck door.

"Willow, if you're reading this then your thankless, good for nothing, drunken whore of a mother has taken you back to Preston and you've either decided you belong in that hellhole, or you've been brainwashed by the other girls and women and those disgusting pedophiles running the place. Now they have you thinking that you actually need them and their 'sanctification' to keep you safe or sane. Whatever. I won't waste good ink to argue about it. Doesn't change the fact that I'm dead now and you've just shat on my last attempt to help you and your ungrateful waste of a mother. You know, I had to kill two men to get away from Preston and one sorry bastard who tried to hurt me on the road as I hitched out of town before I could find a doctor and kill the little monster they'd planted inside me. And when I came back to save your mother, I had to beat my own mother senseless and kill my own father, your grandfather, just to get her out.

You may already know, or you may not, but I'll come clean as it no longer matters. I don't need or want you anymore, you've turned me away for the last time, so here's the truth Willow DeLaCroix. I lied. I knew what would come out of my sister's body so I begged her to have an abortion. I even tried to poison her once, just enough to cause a miscarriage. But you survived. Born sick and frail, but still alive. I tried to

---

kill you once when you were two, at the pool, but one of the mothers found you and got you breathing again. You just wouldn't die. Like Ambrosine.

Later, as you grew, I came to love you and I thought there may be some hope for you. Hope for us. The Tearneys. But now I know I was wrong. There is no Tearney. I made it up, like a little girl playing with dolls.

P.S. I'd say I'll see you in hell, but I'm giving this to you so I won't. I never did touch the damned thing that night I took it off Momma. For what it's worth, I hope you'll kill them all. I hope you bring that whole town down to the ground. You can do it. I've seen it in your eyes girl. And I've heard it in your head.

You're a nightmare.

By the time they gave up yelling through the door and finally kicked it in we'd torn the note into three pieces, each of us eating a piece. The charm was wrapped up and tucked into my underwear, out of sight and safe. But having it there, next to that part of me, gave me chills and made me sweat bullets at the same time. The quarter we'd thrown out the window into the bushes three stories down.

Nails

After the noisy violence of knocking the door in, they didn't seem to know what to do next. Nurse Bell and another nurse eventually eased into the room, taking cautious steps forward and making no sudden movements, as if the three of us were armed and dangerous. They got to work with my pressure and temp again, but didn't ask the other girls to leave my bedside.

Vincent stepped through the busted hole and into the room.

"When a woman shuts her door it means she wants privacy," Ursa sassed.

"We needed to know you girls were alright, and we also need to know what Mr. Goins delivered in that box. I apologize for the lack of privacy, but we do need to see that he didn't bring in something dangerous. Or harmful."

Out in the hallway I spotted Carol.

Ophila spoke up, "You waited till the lawyer was gone and the court advocate was out of sight."

I met Carol's eyes as I spoke to Vincent. "Are you going to have someone else do your dirty work Vincent? Someone easily swayed and desperate to please who will do something they feel is wrong just to be on the team?"

Carol mouthed the words 'I'm sorry' with tears on her face. It looked real, but felt fake, or at least off. Like she was crying because I keep calling her on the fact that she was bitch and not tears because of what she'd done or who she'd hurt. I shook my head as I looked at her. She was a mess.

Vincent followed my gaze then looked back at me. "We know you have an issue with agent Hinze. And I'm not talking about violence Willow."

"I am."

"Its a reasonable request," he ignored my threat. "It's your inheritance. I don't care if it's a jeweled tierra worth fifty million dollars, I'm not going to rob you or take it away unless its a knife or a gun or something obviously hazardous."

"He already knows what it is, or thinks he knows."

"Ophilia, it really is rude to rummage around inside other people's heads uninvited."

"Uninvited?" I pointed to the busted in door and made the face that statement deserved.

"Let's go." Ursa shooed the nurse with the pressure cuff away and started to help me out of bed.

"It's good to see that you've accepted your birthright, though I hope you'll manage your violent tendencies. We don't want accidents and neither do you," Vincent said this as he moved to the side of the room, well out of our way. "When you're ready to hear the truth about your origins, and the history of the Preston Colony that we've unearthed during our investigation, I'll be glad to share it with you. As well as the truth about your namesake, Ambrosine DeLaCroix, and the four nails on the necklace. It will be the unshaded truth as we understand it, and it won't be easy to hear, but it will be the truth."

"We'll be the ones telling her what we are!" snapped Ursa.

"Your version and our version will be different, and Willow will want to hear both. You and Ophilia and the older girls are welcome to hear it as well."

We went back to the cafeteria where all the other girls had gathered together, even the little ones were there. They began to whisper amongst themselves as we entered the room. Now that I knew what I was seeing, I knew what it was. The one's who could hear thoughts where telling those who couldn't something.

"What did you tell them?"

"That you passed the test, and that you have the Nails," answered Ursa.

I began to hear a faint whispering in my head, like many soft voices. It was too soft and varied to sort out the individual voices, but hearing the muddy whispers in my head felt right, not strange.

One of the girls stepped forward. "It don't matter if she passed the test. She's still a murderer and thick in her sin. And she ain't been sanctified."

"She just turned down a fortune to be one of us!" Ursa fired back. "Ophilia and I saw it with our own eyes. All she'd of had to do was give up being a Preston and she'd of been set on easy street!" Ursa shouted back, wanting her words to reach all the girls. "Shut your mouth and pay heed on what I say. Yes, she's killed, but we know from Holly that no one told her what was happening, or why, and Larry and the others didn't have to do things the way they did. We saw how they went after her and each of us has got the same or worse done to us, if not by them then other Preston men, or own own. Strong or not, they got what they had commin. Things are gonna change! The days of being sanctified are over!" she shouted this loudly, tears spilling down her face. "We ain't gonna let men rape us no more!"

"It wasn't rape," one young voice spoke into the quiet, her voice a plea. She gazed around at the other girls asking someone, anyone to tell her it wasn't so.

"Yes it was." a girl near her said quietly.

"It had to end some day," another one said.

"I'm glad Ronicker's dead. I wish I could have killed him myself."

"So what are we gonna do?" asked another girl boldly. "Who's even in charge?"

It was quiet. The older girls glancing toward our keepers, who stood en masse lined up across the back of the room, listening and watching. No one stepped forward. No one wanted to be taken away.

I did what I had to do, and I started with something stupid.

"Only two hours a day of TV for everyone." Heads lifted. Eyes fixed on me. "The little ones will have their TV time in the morning, and the older girls in the evening. And group sessions will be different from now on. One of the older girls will be with each group to see what they're telling or doing with the other girls. And we won't leave the little ones alone with counselors anymore."

"They won't let us do that!" spat one of the girls, "And who put you in charge?!"

"I did. You got a problem with that?" I stared her down.

She dropped her head and shook, no.

"May we see it Willow?" asked a clear, strong voice.

I looked around to see who'd spoken and the girls parted so I could find her. It was the beautiful, blind girl.

"She only looks blind. Tanzy sees through our eyes." Ophila whispered behind me.

I reached down into my scrub pants I still wore from being in the infirmary and pulled the tissue wrapped bundle out of my panties. My throat went dry as I worked at taking the hair scrunchy off that Ursa had wrapped it with to keep the thing together. I carefully peeled back the tissue until it was open there in my hand. I grabbed the leather string the nails were tied to and lifted it up for all the girls to see.

There was a collective intake of breath. A buzz of energy and fear danced in the air all across the room making my own skin crawl. Energy, fear, and excitement.

"I see Ambrosine Reborn!" said one of the twins in a rough scratchy voice, causing girls all across the room to gasp out loud a second time.

"We are sanctified in her!" said the other twin in a voice just as rough and unused as her sisters.

"Then the price has been paid!" shouted a younger girl, eyes aglow with a feral light of madness and hope. She raised her hands, palms out toward me as she dropped to her knees on the cafeteria floor.

"That's just an old wives tale!" shouted Kala Jurvan, "Just a made up story!"

"She's not Ambrosine! She's not even a Preston Girl!" Mitchel's sister Ingrid glared around the room.

"The price has been paid!" a second girl sang out joyfully, ignoring the nasayers. She did the same with her own palms, dropping to her knees.

And then it was all across the room and even the children, all calling out the same, raising their palms to me and going to their knees until even the few who'd at first denied, had joined in. Every Preston Girl except me was kneeling. As one, they began to chant.

"Ambrosine."

"Ambrosine."

"Ambrosine"

"Ambrosine!"

Quietly at first, then louder and louder as I stared at them in absolute horror. It was sad! They were out of their damned minds.

The leather strap and nails floated up into the air and I let go of it and watched, as if in a dream, as it moved over my head then lowered, and lowered, until the nails touched my skin.

The world around me, the cafeteria, and all the chanting voices vanished and were replaced by my own voice crying out as searing pain sang throughout my body, but mostly in my right hand where a nail had been driven straight through my palm.

The Price

I felt her outrage and clung to it for dear life. It was better than panic or fear which was all I wanted to do.

How did I get here?!

How could I get out?!

Get back to..

BASH!

The blow of the hammer crushed those questions as the body I was in jerked and screamed and I screamed along with it, only she screamed in hate more than in pain. Desperately I did the same, only I added my own shock and my furious desire to kill the hammer man to her less directed hate at the world. Hate at what was taken away. We took a deeper breath, our shared rage sustaining us both better than we would have fared alone it seemed.

But what did that mean?

If I could help her, feel her, did that mean I was truly here?

'Ambrosine?'

'Who?'

BASH!

I screamed and forgot that distant life for a moment. That life would not help me now, or her, but what I did have I gave. What help I could offer to this girl I gave. I felt her desire to die, to let go, to give up. I smothered it with my fierce desire to stay alive. We needed to stay alive. She needed to stay alive. For me!

'Is it the Devil?' she thought weakly, wondering who I was.

If she can hear me, then I really am here.

'I'm losing my mind,' the thought floated by just as the hammer came down again on both of us and ripped another shout from our body. For a while we hated, and breathed, and that was all. My desire to live kept us breathing and her hate on behalf of another kept us screaming as the time passed and the nails went in between the poorly aimed blows that crushed our hands and feet.

We screamed, but I felt there was more behind the screams. I felt more. Something deeper. Something that hurt her far worse than all these pains. She screamed at what they'd done to another.

'Yes,' she agreed, 'And it was worth it.' I actually felt her twist our busted and swollen lips into a grim smile.

WHO?

WHO?

WHO is worth this? I had to know! She WAS out of her mind!

In the midst of all this pain and horror, I felt the immensity of her loss and heartache and would have drowned in her sorrow if not for the crushing blow onto our foot that brought us both back with a squeal of shock, and an even more desperate scream in my head.

HER WHO?!

Following my longing obediently, Ambrosine thought of her. Her face was there in my head. Gray eyes. A small, shy smile. Not a supermodel, but pretty. Not brilliant at all, but witty. Forgetful, but always kind. Fun and forgiving. Just a girl. Her secret friend. Her one true confidante. Her secret love. She'd kissed her twice. Only the second time they'd been seen by her father.

That afternoon they'd sold her to a passing noble who'd raped and murdered her in his carriage then threw her out on the side of the road as if she were trash.

Sibyla. Trash..

She'd followed them for three days, killing as she went until she killed the nobleman himself.

'It was worth it. She was worth it.'

A murderous hate, fueled by compassion for a mother I'd never known and love for a girl I'd never kissed, welled up in my soul like a witches brew of mismatched pieces that combined to form something both obscene and somehow holy. This new darkness burst from my lungs and out into the night, not her scream but my own with her mouth. My own black hate steaming out into the frigid night, giving voice to our broken heart. In a voice that was not hers, I cursed the grizzled man holding the hammer.

The hammer man fled, some of the crowd following on his heals disappearing into the night.

I felt a flutter of hope inside our chest that was not of my doing, but then the old priest shouted. We watched as he rallied the frightened men and threatened damnation and other things until they charged forward to finish the work, strong, filthy hands pinching and wrenching our flesh as they rushed, heaving upwards on the heavy wood. A new surge of pain wracked our body as the nails in our flesh and through our bones bore our weight for the first time.

They put us in the ground upside down.

UPSIDE DOWN!

Blood ran down our legs from our pierced feet, down our front joining the blood seeping from the lashes on our back, all of the red streams trickling down to our neck and face and soaking into our long brown hair that dangled all the way to the kindling three feet below.

Ambrosine was outraged. Shocked. Terrified.

'I am pointed straight down to hell!'

'Don't be afraid. You will survive.'

'How do you know? Are you an angel or a devil?'

Thunder boomed overhead making us cry out as the nails hummed down into our bones. The old priest cursed as the superstitious townsfolk threw their torches upon the pyre and fled when the first drops of rain began to fall. Through swollen eyes we watched as the square emptied but for the priest and his one acolyte. The pair exposed their own nakedness as they held their frocks up like a tent over the torches to keep the sputtering flames alive.

Forked lightning flashed, lighting the night. The downpour opened up just at the flames and heat reached our blood soaked hair.

The stink and taste of own blood soaked hair filled our mouth and burned our throat as our frantic body inhaled deeply, inhaling it's own ruin as it sought for life.

There were no more helpful comments. No more time for thought or dialogue across time and space.

We choked on our own ash and screamed out our own burnt blood, tasting our own death as the flames singed our flesh just as the lightning flashed again.

Marks

I woke in my usual bed, in the infirmary, a familiar pain in my hands and feet and a bitter medicine taste in my cotton dry mouth. My stomach rolled. It reminded me of the taste of burnt flesh. Our own. I tried to lift my hands but they didn't move, so I tried to look down at my neck, but couldn't. I didn't feel it on me. It was missing.

I didn't panic.

I looked down the length of the bed, not too alarmed to see that they'd strapped my arms to the rails. It looked clinical and not criminal. It was just some small black velcro straps at the wrists and elbows that held my hands onto pillows someone had put by each rail. The bandages around the backs and palms had a red dot soaking through in the middle of each palm. I could feel that my feet were the same.

Tears filled my eyes until I couldn't see through the watery blur. In my head I saw a girl with gray eyes and a small smile. I tried to recall her voice, but couldn't.

I wasn't mad at Ambrosine, or upset at having been pulled into that hell with her. I'd helped in some way. At least she hadn't been alone. And then there was Sibyla.

'It was worth it,' I agreed as I fought to keep from remembering more of things I didn't wish to remember, as I sought for the things I did. The shakes caught at my shoulders, but I fought for calm. I didn't want it catching hold in my spine. If it got started there I knew they'd be nearly impossible to rid myself of.

"Who is she?"

I froze.

Someone else was in the room. A woman. Not a Preston Girl.

Now that I knew she was there, and obviously poking around inside my head, I recognized the feel of another person in the room with me, and 'inside' me. It was the same as being in the room with Ophilia and the others who had the inside voice,

---

only different. And she wasn't the only thing different. There was something else in the room that pulled at me. I looked to the right. It sat on the shelf by the window were I could see it easily.

"What's in the box? It's locked."

How did she know it was locked? Did she touch it? Try to open it?

Wait. She wanted me to think about it. Wanted a picture of it in my head.

Bitch.

"Bitch? Because I'm curious? That's harsh."

Anger woke me. It gave me strength and a will to fight. Who was this woman anyway?! How long had she been here in my room, poking around in my head. I felt violated while I slept. Raped. It was different to have it done to me by someone other than the Girls. Even the ones who didn't like me I could trust in a way. But not this woman.

"It wasn't rape," she said, serious for the moment. "And now your angry," she complained. "I'm sorry. I guess that may have been a bit rude for you to wake up and find me poking around. Most people never even know I'm there. Sometimes I forget what it's like to be around other powerful psychics. My etiquette may be a bit shitty so let me start over, or I guess, let me start by saying that my name is May Green. Perhaps you've heard of me. I'm famous." she said smugly, trying to be playful and hoping to smooth things over.

I finally looked at her. The tears pooled in my eyes made trails down each cheek as I lifted my head.

I didn't just look, I glared. She thought rape was 'rude'. 'Fair enough', I thought to her not bothering to speak out loud, 'I think murder is merely a matter of time when someone forces themself on me'.

"Yy-yeah. Well, you're in no shape to do me in." She leaned forward and eyed the wreck of me with a scowl. "You know, stigmata isn't all that weird," she said as she tapped her chin with a perfectly manicured nail. "You'd think it was, but it's not. I've seen it a half dozen times myself. Usually it happens to people who are batshit crazy, or crazy devout, like priests and nuns, but sometimes it happens to housewives and kids. I wouldn't let it ruin my day." She reached over to my rolling bedside table and grabbed a soda that had a straw poked in the top that she must have brought in when she came. She took a sip as she eyed me. She was in her thirties or early forties, but dressed like she was in her early twenties. She had an expensive pair of black pants matched with fitted a white top and sharp looking coat. All her clothes looked well to do. Top of the line. Like royalty.

An image of Sibyla's torn and weathered frock as she lay dead in the mud flashed into my head.

"Geez, is that how she ended up? And what the hell was she wearing? Is this a past memory? Past life memories are never that vivid. Okay, that eclipses the stigmata. You're officially starting to weird me out," she complained happily as she put her soda down. "Stop giving me the evil eye, please. I want us to be friends." she sounded sincere but she was still there in my head, forcing, taking what she wanted. "So, who was the girl with the smile? You called her Sibyla. That's French, right?"

I glared, frustrated and furious as she continued to ignore the fact that I felt violated at her being in my head. Did she think I'd just get use to it. Let it happen.

'I want you out of my head.'

"Ease up," she kept up her casually frustrated tone. "I'm not going to hurt you, and unlike the shrinks they'd send in who would load you up on happy pills, I understand that you're not altogether nuts. I'm trying to help Willow. And I really don't see what the big deal is with me seeing, you have thirty or forty others girls – it's more than half of them, right -" she raised her brows at me "you know, ones with the 'voice'." She made finger quotes in the air at the name she'd picked out of my head.

She knew I wanted her to stop, but didn't give a shit. And they had to be listening and watching. They'd sent her in here and by now they knew I wanted her out, but here she sat. I felt other eyes on me and looked around the room. They wouldn't leave this woman in here with me all alone. They'd want to watch the show.

"Like trying to find Waldo in one of those books," she grinned as she watched me search. "You know he's there but your not quiiiite sure where the little bugger is.

Shane Wesley Shelton

It's good to see you using your abilities on purpose and not just latent knee jerk things or incidental stuff that's more like breathing in and out than a deliberate act. Other than mind to mind chatter, all the girls keep it all so bottled in. Just like you. That can't be good for you." She leaned forward then glanced to the door that had been replaced since my last trip to the infirmary. "Of course, being pissed off seems to gives you an edge so that you flex those psychic muscles. And you're pretty pissed right now."

Was she trying to get me to kill her?

Did she think this was a game?

"Come on, I know you're pissed off, but that'll pass once you get over yourself and chill a little. You know, they're not sure if you did the door or the other two who were in here when it happened. Maybe they did it? Have you ever used your abilities on purpose before that door thing yesterday? I can help you get control you know." She gave me a look. "I know you're scared of what you may do. I can feel it. These abilities have nothing to do with God or anything spiritual. They're inherited traits, and you can adjust to having this kind of shit as part of your life without going crazy, because that can happen Willow. And you know..."

I stopped listening to her rambling blather and closed my useless eyes. If the beautiful, blind girl could manage it maybe I could, too. What I was doing was doubly annoying because I had her inside me as I tried to find the camera.

"This is cool to watch by the way. Watching you teach yourself how to parse different fields. Find distinct energies. I can help with that if you want. It's too bad you can't see auras though. That's a neat ability, but crazy rare. What made you decide to close your eyes? ...."

On and on she rambled. Almost as if she were trying to distract me.

I felt it behind me, up high somewhere.

A camera.

"That was quick."

I tilted my head back and looked directly at it. "Get her out. NOW!"

"Willow, I'm sorry for sneaking up on you!" she sat forward, pleading. "Honestly, I know I should have done a proper hello and given some warning, but for real, I didn't know you'd know I was in your head. And dreams are personal, I get that, but I swear I didn't see much. And I know you can tell if I'm lying so you know I'm not. I just walked in here and sat down five minutes before you woke up. All I saw while you were asleep was one nasty dream of you walking in blood, and then you started dreaming about Sibyla. I swear, you started waking up the moment you felt me come in the room. Strong psychics do that even when they're asleep, unless their drunk."

"Or drugged," I said. Remembering the taste on my tongue.

She grimaced. "Yeah. Look, I usually do my act in Vegas, but it's just an act. Mind reading and putzy magic shit for the masses, but from time to time the Feds call me in to help with something they think is important, and I think this is important, too. You're important Willow."

'I don't care why you do it! Or who you are! Or what you think or they think! Get out of my head!'

"It's not a faucet I can turn on and off." She threw her arms out and smiled as she answered my outraged inner cry with a happy carefree tone saying, "I was made this way."

Maybe she thought that if she kept talking long enough I'd get used to having her mind fuck me. Typical behavior for any abuser. Treat the abuse as if it's normal and unavoidable, or even the victims fault, and then just roll with it until they get tired and worn down. Do it until they give you what you want willingly, because they know fighting is useless.

"Right. Past abuse issues. I get that," she gave me a sad look, as if I were damaged. "I'm not trying to mess with your head or abuse you, I want to get to know you Willow. And I may not be a Preston Girl, but this is how I was born. I'm like you, and you might as well use it to help you and the other girls." She reached for the box of tissues on the table and dabbed at her eyes.

"I really am here to help."

I smiled at her act, unmoved by her words or her crocodile tears as I let myself sink into that determined place I went to when I was backed into a corner and had no other choice. I tried to lift my hands, but the straps held. But then.. I didn't really need my hands. There were things I could do without hands.

But if I did that, and the same thing happened..

Without meaning to, I thought of the quarter.

May sat up, a distant look in her eyes that didn't match the horror struck expression on her face.

"Oh my God! What the hell did you do to that quarter?" her voice was different this time. More herself. Less show and nice. No more playful annoyance.

I looked at her. Thought to her.

'I touched it without my hands May. I touched it like your touching me now.' In the same way I'd done with my mother, I imagined killing her as I stared at her, picturing - or trying to - what might happen to the head I was staring at if I touched it. I'd slit Garvy's throat and I'd blown Larry's brains out the back of his head, but I still didn't feel I had the imagination to do this justice, but then again, I really wouldn't need imagination soon. I'd see it for real.

The unwanted presence in my mind vanished.

May got slowly to her feet, eyes carefully averted and fixed on the ground, her face pale as a sheet.

"Mrs. Green, are you alright?" Vincent's concerned voice spoke over the speakers set by the bed used for the nurse to answer when I pushed the call button.

'Run liar, before I touch you and show you how I was made.'

She was out of the room in a flash.

I laid back in the bed and closed my eyes and spoke out loud, talking as if someone was still in the room. Because there was.

"Please don't do that again Vincent. And don't send her, or others like her to the young girls who might not know what's happening. That's what a pedophile would do...start with the young girls who might not know what's what and rape an innocent mind."

"We haven't sent May or anyone like her to anyone but you Willow. And even if we did, it wouldn't be to harm them." His voice came across the speakers by my bed again.

"Did you hurt May?" he asked.

"Almost."

"You're going to have to control your violent tendencies Willow. We messed up. This was poorly handled. May assured us you wouldn't know she was inside your thoughts. And she should have left when you asked her to. And I know we should have asked her to leave when you told us to, but we were holding out hope that she could make some kind of connection with you. But killing someone who's trying to help you, even if you don't want that help, is not acceptable. What she did was invasive and we - I - am partly to blame for that. But we are not rapists or abusers. We are tying to help you and the other girls Willow."

His logic was ugly.

"So if May was able to do what she wanted, without me waking or knowing, you'd have been fine with it. You must think it's okay to rape someone's mind of whatever's in there if they don't know it's happening, or if you can make them forget that it happened after the fact with drugs or some other mind game shit?"

"In our defense, you seemed liberal with your mental privacy. We had no idea it would.."

"I'm done talking to you on this thing!" I cut in rudely. Why wasn't he in the room talking to me? Was he worried I'd hear him lying?

"Remove this camera and all the other cameras in the other girls rooms!" I ordered. "And if I find one in a bathroom," I growled threateningly, "one that we girls use, I swear to God you'll pay for it with blood, Vincent. Your blood, not someone else's. Or is bathroom privacy the same to you as mental privacy? If we don't know your looking at our bare tits and asses then its no harm no foul."

"Willow, you should be focused on taking care of yourself. You don't have to be a mother to these girls. I know you had an unusual experience yesterday and I don't mean to discount it, but you shouldn't feel as if you're responsible or in any way.. .."

I sat bolt upright, straining against the straps as I shouted at the top of my lungs.

"SHUT! UP! SHUT! UP! SHUT! UP! SHUT! UP! SHUT! UP! SHUT! UP!"

I screamed out each word as if it were a knife I was plunging into his chest. I screamed until I couldn't see anything but dots. I screamed until I fell back into the bed, panting and faint.

I heard the door and opened my eyes as the nurse and four of the younger Preston Girls rushed in.

'Are you alright,' a young girl with curly, red hair who looked like a sister to the twins asked very loudly in my head.

I smiled at her weakly, amused.

"Ambrosine?" another girl asked as she leaned in close and peered into my eyes as if there may be some other person hiding inside my head. She was a year older that the red head, and had long, straight, black hair and lovely, almond colored eyes that were tilted the slightest bit. They reminded me of my own eyes, when I bothered to look into a mirror. I'd heard one of the girls calling her 'Daf'. Short for Daphne? I wondered how closely we were related? Behind her two other girls whispered together shyly.

"I'm Willow right now," I rasped through my abused throat as Nurse Bell went about her work on my hands and feet which had sprung fresh leaks, messing the pillows and sheets.

The girls gathered around my bed, making room for Bell as she worked on me, even helping with the bandages and holding things for her like little assistant nurses. They began touching me and stroking my hair, shyly at first and then more surely. They started to take turns humming. They hummed as I lay there and breathed, and wondered what I was doing and why I was doing it. Second guessing what I'd said to Vincent until I got stuck thinking on something May had said to me. What if I was just losing it? Crazy people get stigmata. Was this really happening as I thought it was or was I losing it? Had I really been crucified upside down and burnt on a cross with Ambrosine? Had I spoken to her? Was it a memory, or had it been real? And Sibyla, was she real? Just the thought that she might not be hurt my heart, but still, I considered it as a possibility.

Had I really done that to the quarter? I hadn't actually seen it happen. I just opened my eyes and it was squished. Maybe someone switched it when my eyes were closed.

But I'd been alone.

'You ain't got the out loud voice, but you'd have felt someone in your room,' said the redhead's inside voice as she drew her breath to hum.

'She's got a little of it,' said another voice shyly. One of the others.

What about the door? Was it me, or was it Ursa and Ophilia? And if it was me, what did that mean? What did all of this mean? A few weeks ago I was just a girl in school trying to get through the day and hoping to find a substitute for my hopeless crush on Lynn Young. My biggest aggravation was dealing with a drunk mother who might bring home a sicko.

How did I get from there to here?

What the hell was Preston, and why were we all this way?

They didn't answer, they just stood around my bed and hummed and stroked my hair while Bell redid bandages. I felt them there, inside my head. Those young eyes, eyes that could see all the swirling confusion inside my head, watched me inside and out as I slipped down into sleep.

Recovery Days

As it turned out, I wasn't the only one who'd had enough of Vincent and his games. The Preston Girls united and asserted themselves, casting out the watchers that lurked around the edges of the rooms, destroying cameras and taking charge of their own care and of me and my mine while Vincent and Dr. Doughtry backed off, letting them rule themselves almost completely. I wasn't out there to see it for myself, but I was kept informed as if I had a right to know. I was told that they'd done as I'd instructed, limiting TV time for the younger and older girls to two hours a day. Private counseling remained in place for the older girls, but they'd ended up going much farther with the group session reforms than adding 'observers'. They told Vincent that they wanted Mrs. Kathy and the other group leaders gone, and they wanted him to bring in some of the missing Preston mothers to run the group sessions. In private. No cameras or watchers. He'd agreed to it, provided they agreed to end the long standing silence and actually 'talk' and share with one another. The girls watching over me were excited and full of their own opinions as they described what sounded like an open forum debate that took place in the cafeteria where the Preston Girls discussed which mothers they wanted and who'd be best and who wouldn't.

A group of girls headed by Ursa had come into my room after the meeting to assure me that no mother would be invited into the group who didn't fully accept me as Ambrosine Reborn. They hadn't asked for my permission or approval for this, they'd simply informed me how it was. I'd only had to nod and even the nod wasn't truly needed. They were jealous of their newfound devotion and wouldn't tolerate anyone trying to poke at it, except me oddly enough, and my poking didn't even convince myself and only seemed to strengthen their own convictions. I didn't think I was everything they said or hoped I was, but I couldn't help but fear I was much more than just the 'Willow' I'd been for the past sixteen years. I couldn't deny what had happened to me, that I'd been there with her, and that what I'd seen and felt had been real. Even more strange was knowing that Ambrosine had been gay, like me. That she'd loved a girl. A love I'd felt, been in ardent favor of and even now regretted and mourned the loss of. And of course, she'd been a murderer, like me. The coincidences rolled around inside my head constantly as the girls around me listened and watched me think and worry as I ate a strawberry,

---

then paused to wonder if Ambrosine had liked them, too. Did I like them because she had?

Any time my mind tried to rationalize and explain things away in part or in whole, those seeds of doubt would only endure until they changed my bandages. It was all I could do not to get the shakes each time I saw the scabbed over holes, as I fought to not relive the nails pushing in and the clumsy hammer blows, the flames climbing up our hair like a bloody wick as we hung upside down and watched the fire come closer and closer while we screamed. The angry sky above a violent mirror of the flames below as thunder rolled and lightning flashed as if God were screaming, too.

Screaming with us, or at us I wondered.

As for the Preston Girls who were changing those bandages, my fear that I wasn't 'Willow' and my dread that I might be Ambrosine Reborn was a hundred times more convincing for them than if I'd come out waving a flag, campaigning for the title. I didn't try to hide my own confusion and fear or my frustration as I laid in the infirmary recovering from my chronic case of stigmata. And I didn't pull punches when I answered their questions or shy away from the occasional screaming freak out. I even attempted one moody pity party for myself, though my heart wasn't in it and I ended up playing a board game with the children they sent in when I'd chased the older girls out so I could pout. I'd never been big on pity, even for myself. And even as I'd shouted and tried to cry as I told them to get the hell out, they knew I didn't really mean it or wish to be alone. They also knew I would never be mean to a child for no reason.

As for being gay, now that they knew Ambrosine had been gay it wasn't seen as a problem, but as a token of confirmation. A sign. And more, though I'd avoided questions about the whole 'she is our sanctification' thing, I knew my being gay figured into this equation as well. Whatever. I was gay. I didn't let their hang ups make me feel self conscious in those rare moments of desire when one of the girls in my room caught my eye. There wasn't any way I could hide what I was feeling or thinking even if I'd wanted to, so I didn't try to. Though, with the girls taking turns as my helpers and me stuck in my bed till my feet got better, even if I did see a girl I liked I wouldn't see her again for days.

They rotated in two hour shifts, with four girls in my room at all times with at least two of those with the voice, so there was no privacy or private thought for me at any time for any reason. For someone who'd been a loner all her life, aloof even from those I considered my friends, you'd think this situation would've driven me nuts, but to my own surprise I found that I didn't miss the privacy at all. I felt as if I'd stood in a room by myself for sixteen years, loved and cared for by no one but me, able to trust no one but me, and now I had almost seventy other girls in that room with me. Girls who cared for me and were related to me - like sisters. It frightened me how much I liked it. Liked this. Wanted to keep it. I'd only been with the Preston Girls for ten days and I could already see how incredibly hard it would be for any girl who'd grown up this way to ever leave.

One of the strangest things was how the children seemed like little adults most of the time. A four year old with the voice could look at you and be empathetic even if they didn't understand the reasoning behind your issue. This also meant they knew which adults or older girls might be dangerous or simply didn't want them around and which ones didn't mind. They could 'think out' those welcome laps to crawl into or the few who wanted a non complicated hug, even if they were too proud or embarrassed to admit it. The young girls without the voice were usually good at sensing moods so they weren't too handicapped, and these girls were always paired with another girl her own age who would be her 'whisper sister'. Ophilia said she'd love to be mine, but that it wouldn't have been fair to the others. And I didn't need my own whisper sister as I was never alone in my room. Even when I slept. There was even arguing between the girls over who'd get to watch me at night as my dreams and the glimpses seen there had become items of great interest.

Nightmare Visitation

I woke from a nightmare panting and out of breath, but I couldn't recall why.

Two shadowed figures were standing beside my bed. Two girls in the darkened room, watching over me, and I could see well enough to know they were both on the verge of tears. I wondered how long they'd been standing there and not seated. A chill took me as a bead of cold sweat trickled down my back. I grabbed a pillow from behind me and hugged it tight to help hold myself together as my teeth started chattering.

"It was Sibyla," Meriemalee whispered.

'What about her?' I wondered.

Angela, the other Preston Girl in the room, answered my thought out loud.

"Ambrosine killed all those people for Sibyla. And you killed for Mel. Do you love Mel?"

Did I love her? Instead of brushing it aside, I gave the question a moment of deeper consideration as I sat there in my bed, sweat chilled from my troubling dream. The clock on the wall said 2:15 A.M. The room sat in shadows. It seemed a safe place to think through unsafe thoughts.

Love. It didn't get much more 'unsafe' than that.

Did I love Mel?

Here I sat, in the dark, in the dead of night, but I hadn't been alone in it. I'd had a bad dream, but these two had been there with me. And they'd been here, standing by my bed and watching over me when I woke. Tears welled in my eyes as I thought of all those lonely frightening nights I'd endured with a drunken mother, who wouldn't have been able to wake even if I'd screamed bloody murder let alone care to help if she had been awake. And if I'd woke in the night to find someone beside my bed

---

it would have been one of her shit boyfriends come to rape me or kill me and not someone who loved me and cared for me.

Tears ran down my face. I wished my mother had never taken me away from Preston, but at the same time, I was glad she had or I wouldn't be me. And if she hadn't taken me away Preston would still be a hellhole and the girls wouldn't be free.

Did I love Mel? I did, but not just her. I loved them all. I loved the Preston Girls. They were my family.

Meriemalee smiled at me in the dark, but my other, young dream watcher shook her head of long, dirty blond hair. "No, not that kind of love. That's not what I'm talking about. Have you been with her? Have you had sex with her?"

I sobered, sat up and studied the child. Sweet little Angela,only ten years old. She wore an intense expression as she waited for an answer, weighing bloody murder and sexual issues far beyond what a girls her age should be able to comprehend.

Meriemalee stepped forward and put an arm around Angela. Her smile for me was now a frown and her voice was protective and a bit angry, "She can comprehend it just fine. She knows what sex is. Angela began being sanctified by her father, and others, when she was nine. They're supposed to wait until we're thirteen at the least, but most don't."

I sat bolt upright in bed and stared in horror at Meriemalee, then at sweet little Angela's innocent, young face and her suddenly trembling bottom lip. Only her tremble wasn't from a chill. I didn't need the voice to see the memories of torments past as they flashed by in her eyes.

A black rage hit me like I'd been struck by lightning. I threw my head back and screamed for all I was worth. It was the same unearthly scream as I'd unleashed on the hammer man and the crowd around our cross. The scream came from not just my lungs, but from inside myself, filling the room, knocking all the little things about, throwing open the doors and filling the hall and touching those there, not just emotionally but physically.

I let the scream die, dazed and absolutely freaked out by the odd sensation and at an absolute loss to describe what I'd just experienced. The vase on the window sill, the tissue box, the cup and little stuff on my rolling bedside table were everywhere. Angela and Meriemalee, looking wide eyed and windblown, were watching me with cautious eyes from the far side of the room. Cautious, but not afraid. Other girls were coming at a run, their socks and the slick tile in the hall causing them to miss the door altogether or slide to an unsteady halt if they made a lucky grab at the frame. They gathered there just long enough to take in the scene or sense what was happening before stepping into the room and dropping to their knees with cries of "Ambrosine! Ambrosine!"

"What's happened? Let us through! Girls! Move!" I heard Nurse Bell shouting out in the hall.

Angela hadn't knelt like the rest, she'd come closer and now stood by my bedside watching me.

'Ambrosine?' I heard her ask through lips that hadn't moved.

Was I still me? Was she here now?

Was the girl from the cross here with me?

WHAT THE HELL JUST HAPPENED!

"Is she Ambrosine?"

I didn't know myself. My head hurt, and my skin felt funny and I wanted out of it.

"We are your children. All of us," said one of the girls from the murmuring crowd packed into the room.

Had Ambrosine been one of their ancestors?

One who was burned for being a witch?

Heads around me nodded and I tried to think on the implications of that with my fuzzy head as I scratched at the prickles running up and down my arms when an older woman, who had to be one of the mothers, pushed through the kneeling girls and glared at us.

"They aren't your children! They're ours! Be gone, Devil!" she shouted at me. "You'll not have our daughters!"

I blinked at the accusation, not getting it, but one thing didn't escape me. She was a mother of a Preston Girl. My eyes moved to Angela's concerned, young face and the reason for my psychotic scream flared to life within me as I turned and glared at the 'mother'. My voice was raw and horse as I spoke.

"You did nothing as a nine year old was raped by the men of Preston!" I let the disgust I felt show on my face, "And why would you lift a hand to help Angela when you allowed your own children to be raped. Ambrosine's children! MY SISTERS!" I hissed. "What good are you?"

The wild eyed woman turned imploring eyes onto the girls around her. I didn't hear her voice, but I felt a murmuring. Words I couldn't quite make out were there in my head. Though I hadn't heard, somehow I got the impression she wanted to do to me what they'd done to 'that girl'.

"You want to crucify me?" I guessed.

She reared back in guilty surprise. I sneered, "Been there. Done that. Got the T-Shit!" I held up my hands for her to see. My screaming cry had broken open my wounds enough to sprout red dots in the middle of my bandaged palms.

The mother's they'd brought in for group had never seen me or my wounds. She stared in fixed horror at the red on my hands. She said nothing, but I saw the devious intent in her eyes. This time I closed my own eyes and concentrated as hard as I could, and the murmuring skipped in and out of focus, forming words in my head.

'She ... hear.. . Willow has... .... can kill with a thought, but .... voice. Don't speak .... be deceived by the marks. She's nothing but a devil. We must burn her. I..................... we must!'

"You wont kill a Preston man for raping your daughters, but you'll kill me for killing to save them." I glared as her bottom jaw dropped open, then in a screw you, raw and ravaged voice that actually sounded evil and demon possessed I added, "And if burning didn't kill us the first time, what the fuck makes you think it would work now?"

Unexpected laughter burst from my throat at hearing what I'd just said, and at the look on her face. I laughed as fresh tears ran down our face.. her face?.. my face? Memories of burning flashed in my head. The taste of our own burnt flesh. The fire. The nails. Ambrosine.

Who was Ambrosine?

Who was I?

It was all too much to take. The room began to spin in circles. I fell back into the bed exhausted, numb, drifting in the murmuring sea of voices all around us until a needle found our arm and darkness claimed us.

Reap the Whirlwind

It seemed this latest visitation had pushed things a bit far for Vincent's comfort level, either that or things had simply gone beyond his pay grade. This morning when I woke the girls told me there were some new people at the facility, though Vincent still seemed to be the one in charge. He hadn't interfered with the girls' management, but their was more security around that they could see out the windows and guards had been posted within the facility. They also wanted access to me, which the girls had forbidden for the past eight days.

Viki and Holly had just helped me into a wheelchair when the door opened and three people entered our room.

I glared, suddenly furious. I could have been undressed and they hadn't even knocked!

"Don't slam it!" Holly whispered to me, shaking her head.

"Why didn't you knock?" scolded Gemma, bringing the smiling group to a sudden stop just inside the door. Out in the hallway a light flickered and then popped. A man outside the door, who looked like a guard, shielded his head and eyes from the rain of falling glass as he ducked into the room.

Our unwanted guests only glanced at me before zeroing in on Gemma, who now stared at the floor, as the source. They gave her appraising looks while also taking in the sympathetic looks directed her way by Viki and Elisabeth.

"More accidents?" asked Vincent, as if he weren't surprised at the incident.

"More?" I looked around at the girls, brows bunched in worry, but no one would meet my eye.

Holly stood behind me and whispered into my ear.

"Gemma has always had a problem with lights when she gets angry. And some of the other girls have been having problems. Three have the fever. One of the girls broke all the TV's yesterday. Other little things, too. Nothing huge." Her voice was meant to be reassuring, but I felt her unease.

"Hello, Willow." A new woman, who'd come in with Vincent, gave me a tight grin that crinkled the corners of her eyes as Vincent and another man behind her kept tight lipped, concerned smiles in place letting her speak. "I'm sure by now you've heard there's been a bit of a change up in our management here. My name is Delia Borrows. I'm a paranormal psychologist and researcher and I work with the government. This is Senator Borden Reeves, he's here to ensure your rights are being respected and that the interest of the state of Pennsylvania and its children are being taken to heart. Some, many actually," she amended, "are concerned that the government will try to take advantage of you girls because of your unique heritage and psychic abilities."

"And are you saying that those people are wrong?" I asked.

"No, not at all." she admitted easily. "They would have stolen you away and made up a convenient story in a flash back when this first happened, but they didn't realize what they had until it was beyond their ability to hide under a covert blanket. This didn't happen in a closet Willow, and people like the senator and the millions of other Americans who've seen a piece of that video you uploaded have made the Preston Girls quite safe from invasive government shenanigans." She cracked a smile and let out a big breath, "God, it's so nice to actually be able to say who I am and what I do without all double talk and hush hush bull. It's quite liberating. I imagine that's part of the appeal of being with the Preston Girls."

Holly leaned to my ear. "Can you hear me right now Ambrosine?" she whispered into my ear. She pointed to the senator and the other man in a suit with a delicate finger. "They're both trying to think of a blank piece of paper." But what caught my eye wasn't those two, but the gloves that the man who'd been out in the hall had on. Why would he be wearing gloves?

'Get the nails from the box,' I thought to them.

Gemma met my eyes, my own suspicions mirrored there. She turned and headed to the window. The box hadn't been locked when they'd returned the nails to their usual resting place last night.

Delia's smile brightened, eyes flaring with interest as if I'd done something impressive.

"How did you know we were going to look in the box?"

"The same way I know your geneticist wants our DNA and to harvest our eggs so he can cross them with a monkey just to find out if he can teach it to peel bananas without using hands." I glared up at her, "You're a scientist, right?"

"Yes," she admitted cautiously.

"Then your curiosity and need to know is more important to you than my privacy, and," I made finger quotes, "'the greater good of all mankind' will always win out over the rights of one girl or one group of girls."

She gave me a twisted smile, I guess she meant to look amused. "You've obviously read a lot of fantasy and science fiction Willow. And watched a lot of movies about the evils of the government. That's fantasy, not reality. You have rights. Just because your gifted doesn't change that."

Senator Reeves spoke up, his voice deep and sincere. "Willow, I'm here to make sure the people at this facility respect your privacy and your rights, but we also want to help. Vincent and Nurse Bell spoke with us this morning and they don't think the girls have told you how bad things are getting for the others." He directed a meaningful glance toward Gemma then continued. "They tell me all the Preston Girls can sense when someone is lying or being manipulative, so we want to be as forthcoming as we possibly can. No one is going to force you to do anything you don't wish to be a part of, but we do want to help. And you apparently need our help."

My head was spinning with questions, and worries. But one thing was certain, the moment we accepted help from these people that would be an admission that we couldn't take care of ourselves. It would open the door to all the rest of the hell they so wanted to do to us under the label of 'its for your own good'.

But what to do? What could I do?

Fevers..

"Which girls have the fever heat?" I demanded of Viki sharply.

"Ursa, Lisa Marie, and Angela," she answered right away.

I'd wondered where Ursa had gone to. And I'd never seen a girl named Lisa Marie. She must have been one of the ones avoiding me. But little Angela? She had seemed a bit off last night. Almost desperate, now that I thought about it. And she'd been so very insistent on knowing about me and Mel and... sanctification.

Why was this happening? And what could I do? What did they need?

"Take me to them," I said, my mind still running but getting nowhere.

Holly took the brake off the chair and began to roll me forward.

"Gemma, come with me. And bring the nails."

"What are you gonna do?!" asked Holly in a frazzled squeak at my ear.

The three adults and the glove wearing guard still stood in front of the doorway. Delia spoke for the unmoving roadblock.

"The last time you came into contact with those nails you almost died Willow. I don't think you should touch them again, or at least, not until you know about Louise Partan and John Preston."

"Get out of my way," I warned.

"I promise, we will," she wasn't lying, "but before you put that thing back on and have another religious episode I want you to know what we know and then at least whatever happens will be tempered by that knowledge."

"It won't take long. I just watched it myself," assured the senator.

"It's fifteen minutes long," supplied Vincent.

"They've put together a video, to make it easier to take in, though it is grim stuff so.."

Holly spoke. "They want you to take something to keep you calm. They're afraid you might hurt yourself or someone else if you don't."

I frowned, then turned and looked back at Holly because she sounded sincere, not flip. And the look I found on her face, if anything, was on their side.

"It might be best," said Viki softly.

Gemma held the nails and looked too hungry for whatever help might be forthcoming to care either way. No matter what. She looked right at me and nodded, unashamed of her need.

Seeing that need, and the hope Gemma had in me, broke my heart.

'I'd die for you Gemma. I'd kill for you. And I'll put on the nails and be Ambrosine for you if that's what it takes.' I thought to her. 'And if the only way to help you is to sanctify you, I'll do that too. If you want.' For a brief moment the similarities between Gemma and Sibyla played across my mind. Both pretty, but in an average way. Similar quirky smiles, build, height and they even had the same twisty, naturally curly, brown hair. Both were easy going..

"Are they communicating mind to mind?"

The senator's deep voice and the back and forth replies from Vincent and Diane freed me of my daydreaming spell. I looked away from a wide eyed Gemma and studied the floor, my heart racing. I felt hot again. I so didn't need that. I counted tiles on the floor in a four square circle, trying to calm down.

"May we give you something?" asked Delia. "Nothing too strong, just something to help your control."

'Nineteen', 'Twenty'.. I looked up and glared at her. "I'm not having accidents like the others. And I've never killed or hurt anyone on accident."

Surprised faces regarded me. They quickly schooled their expressions to guarded sympathy, but they'd already let the cat out of the bag.

Holly spoke, out loud for my and Viki's benefit. "That day your mother took you to the liquor store there were other people there. In the store. Two. One of the sheriff's men and the owner of the store died that day with your mother."

I listened, but what I was hearing didn't make sense. "I would have heard about other people dying. I saw some TV while I was in the hospital."

Vincent answered it. "The sheriff kept the other two deaths out of the news."

"But it wasn't me!" I glared. "I could hardly stand! I had a concussion!"

"After your mother turned and slapped you, every bottle in the store burst and the flying glass filled the aisles like a swarm of bees cutting them and your mother many, many times."

"But, I was falling.."

The others were watching me as Vincent carefully shook his head. "You fell, but you never hit the ground Willow. You remained levitating about two feet off the floor in the aisle as the store imploded and became a storm of glass. Not one piece of which hit you," he added before I could argue that point. "There were security cameras in the store. We have the whole thing on video, but its not anything you should see. It's enough to know that it happened. And to know that you have had accidents. Deadly ones."

The deputy had to be a Preston man, and from the way the store owner had looked at me and my mother, I knew he had been one too.

The deputy.. the liquor man.. they'd been coming to take me.

Oh well.

"I still won't take your pills, but I'll watch whatever it is you want me to watch."

"It doesn't bother you that two innocent men died?" asked Diane, eyeing me as if she were weighing my moral character. Judging my callousness and capacity for murder.

"What was the deputy's name?"

"Capillano. Officer Nathan Capillano."

I gripped the wheels of my chair and turned it to face the three girls.

"The liquor store man or Deputy Nathan ever sanctify any of you three?"

Holly looked away, but nodded. Gemma looked uncomfortable, but shook her head no, as did Viki.

I rolled my chair back around and glared at the four, grim faced adults before me. I spoke to the girls at my back and to the ones still barring my way forward. "Viki, I want you to go through the girls we have here and gather all the ones who were ever sanctified by those two. Gather them in the cafeteria and then clear out the rest." I sharpened my eyes on Vincent. "You're right by the way, I don't need to see it, but there's girls here that do. You get that video from the liquor store. I'll watch what you've put together for me as they watch that. And don't edit out the blood or the screams," I said darkly. "I'm sure they didn't edit anything they did to these girls, and the end of someone evil should be something three times as evil."

"Sow the wind and reap the whirlwind," said Holly. "I'd like to see him die."

They stood there, the senator, Delia, Vincent and the FBI guard, if that was what he was, all of them looking at us with pained expressions as if they didn't know what to do next.

"Showing them violence will only cause harm," said Delia.

"Is that what you people call closure now? Harm?" I challenged, making them blink. "You'd rather show a video of the Preston men laughing and playing board games together, or out in the yard gardening, or crying in group over what they'd done and how bad they feel about it?"

"How many of the girls did those two rape?" asked the senator darkly.

"It'll be a crowded room," Holly said, wiping at her eyes. "Now get that video!"

John Preston

The video that they wanted me to see started like a classroom documentary, centered on a page out of an old book that showed the sketch of a Frenchman with the larger than life hat complete with feathers and a puffy collared shirt, while a narrator, whose voice I didn't recognize, spoke in a clinical, emotionless tone as she described the horrors that were the origins of my history. It started with some basics on the dark ages and the start of the witch trials and how before they became hated and hunted, many nobles in France had sought out witches and tried to marry them and use them as they ruled. This practice of marrying and using witches ended when the church began its persecution of witchcraft in the thirteenth and fourteenth century, but a few powerful families still sought witches for their own ends, but they did so in secret.

In 1456, a young Louise Partan traveled to the middle east to study the Arabian methods of horse breeding. He became intrigued by the idea of selective breeding of horses to develop specific traits. At great expense, he purchased five Arabian mares and a stallion to bring back to France to crossbreed with their existing stock, whose progeny would be the primary source of the Partan's family fortunes in the many years to come. But Louise also had other plans for this newfound knowledge. Plans that involved human breeding to develop specific traits.

When he returned to France, Louise and his father publicly denounced all witchcraft and affirmed a new commitment to God and joined in the religious persecution which was sweeping across Europe and England. Partan enlarged a neglected monastery in his province, installed his own priests and sent them out to hunt for women accused of witchcraft. Through the darkest years of the witch hunts the Priests of Partan traveled throughout France, Germany, Spain, Belgium, England and Turkey taking pilgrimages as far away as Russia and even attempting one failed expedition into India seeking women who were 'real' witches. They inspected thousands, but of those accused of witchcraft they found only a sparse handful who could pass even one of three holy tests. Lighting a candle unaided, moving a coin untouched, or passing various card and mind reading games. Those who failed were either pardoned or summarily burned as a witch, while those few who passed were purchased from their fate and almost certain execution with thirty coins of the region of varying amounts, but in every case one of those coins was given back to the purchased witch as a token of her sin, and a sign of her redemption by the Partan Priesthood.

Through the fifteenth and early sixteenth centuries the Partans' fortunes grew, but they still kept to themselves and always stayed one step ahead of their enemies and the ever shifting winds of political and religious power, shifting allegiance and faiths as times demanded. Through it all, the Partan Priests continued their witch hunts until the end of the sixteenth century, when Johannes Louise Partan fled in the middle of the night with what remained of the familie's fortune, leaving his playboy brother - who'd brought on their downfall - and his 'Public' wife behind to face execution as he and the Partan Priests slipped away into England by ship, carrying his stolen inheritance of fifty prize horses and a collection of women and children.

There was much persecution of fringe religions at this point in history, and most of these groups were fleeing England and most of Europe for the religious freedom in the New World - the Americas. William Penn had just started the Pennsylvania Colony and had declared it a place of true, religious freedom.

Wearing a priests robes and calling himself Bishop John Preston, Johannes Louise Partan used his new identity and stolen inheritance to purchase the Preston Colony from King Charles II. Without delay, he chartered two ships with the last of his wealth and set sail for a new home and a new kingdom.

In Pennsylvania they started the Preston Settlement, but unlike the Quakers in Philadelphia or the Germans who settled Germantown, the Prestonians did not welcome outsiders into their community or encourage visitors. They kept to themselves. The practices of selective breeding of women with unique talents that the priests had instituted over the many centuries continued, with its history and practices merged and mingled with religious doctrine and tempered by the harsh demands of life in a wilderness colony.

An old black and white drawing of few dozen, wooden homes surrounded by a wooden fence faded into a modern day picture of Preston as the story continued. The image on the flat screen TV faded from the freeze frame aerial view of modern day Preston to a moving video of men who looked like police or the FBI as they entered Preston City Hall. The camera followed the men, the view bouncing up and down as they passed down halls and through door after door, all with cut locks that now dangled uselessly, their secrets no longer safe. On they went until they reached an ominous looking room with nothing but a stairway that lead downward. At the bottom of the stair was a room with shelves of books and other items that looked ancient.

The narrator began to explain what was being shown, telling how the histories of the Prestonians were brought with them in the ships. The histories described how the priests and women of Preston lived during the two hundred and twenty six years of captivity in Parton France, and how they lived during the three hundred and twenty eight years since forming the Prestonian Colony in 1685. While in the Partan Monastery, each male child born of the women would have taken on the last name of the priest who'd fathered the child. Those male children would have been removed from their mothers and raised by wet nurses, who were not gifted, until weaned. According to their teachings and the attempts at genetic engineering set in place by Louise Partan, these children when grown would assume the priesthood themselves and would be assigned a group of women to 'sanctify' with their seed. These girls and women would be carefully selected to avoid close genetic ties. Each girl child born would be tested to see if she'd inherited the 'gift' or 'gifts' of the mother. If the child did not pass any of the tests by the age of thirteen she would be taken away and burned and the bones then interred in the Monastery. The surnames of the women were handed down to their gifted daughters. These practices continued from 1458 to 1684 with new women being brought in during the witch hunts periodically to freshen the gene pool as the sons of the women in captivity became their jailers, their priests, the fathers of their children and the murderers of their ungifted female children, their own daughters and sisters.

The camera and the live shot had ventured deeper by this point, past that one room and downward into what looked like ancient catacombs. Catacombs, right here in Preston, not on the other side of the ocean in an old ruin. I didn't blink as the camera passed over stone shelves that held human skulls, beneath each skull were carefully arranged piles of bones. Skeletons. I watched numbly as the narration continued to describe how the practice of disposing of ungifted offspring continued here in Preston, and here the voice of the narrator finally managed something close to an emotion as she said that mercifully almost every child born in the past two hundred years had been born with one or more gifts. Those few who did not pass the test were killed and added to the rest of the dead. The recent Prestonian records indicate that in the past twenty years nine young girls ages twelve to fourteen had been murdered as had forty eight male children who'd been killed at birth. Fewer males alive in Preston meant that there were more women for the ones who were left. According

Shane Wesley Shelton

to the records, the women were so fearful of their daughters being born weak or without the gift that they were more than willing to let the male infants of weakly gifted women die in hopes that a stronger woman in the power would give birth to a stronger son and then a stronger child for them to keep as their own daughters.

The breakdown of the system began during the sixties and seventies when the town's mineral wealth and high real estate values in other parts of the state caused uncontrolled growth and non Prestonian movement into the valley. Despite the communities efforts to isolate, access to information due to modernization introduced new ideas and challenged their centuries old belief systems. The death of last direct descendent of Louise Partan in 1999 ended the high priesthood and further weakened the religious elements of the community. Ultimately, the system of selective breeding for specific traits that Louise Partan began almost six hundred years earlier ended January 28th, 2016.

Prophecy Revealed

I woke in the infirmary with the sick taste of vomit still in my mouth mixed with whatever drugs they'd give me, not knowing how I got there. I looked around for the girls and felt a moment of dread to find that no one was in the room with me. It had been so long since I'd been alone it frightened me.

I slipped out of bed and tiptoed to the front door, testing out my feet for the first time on something bigger than the short trip to the bathroom. It hurt, but I managed to get there without falling over. I heard voices just outside so I put my ear to the new - much more sturdy - metal door, but this time instead of just trying to listen to their voices I tried to hear that faint whisper that was usually too soft to understand. I tried to make it happen like it had with the Preston mother who wanted me burned, but each time I went to match up the sound in my head to the sound outside my head, they'd slip apart again.

I couldn't do it.

Maybe I could only hear the stronger Preston girls, and whoever was out there probably wasn't a witch. If I were one of the girls with the voice I could do it. I bet Ambrosine could have done it..

I looked over to the window ledge, and the old box.

Should I?

Would she?

What's the worse that could happen? I get sucked back into the past and burn with her? Or maybe if I did go back, I could help her more. Stop things earlier, or if she came here instead she could help me hear whoever was on the other side of this door. Excited, afraid, and gritting my teeth against the pain in my feet, I tottered over to the window shelf. I tried the lid, but the box was locked, as I knew it would be. But if I called one of the girls with the key I'd give myself away. My heart raced as I considered the other option. I didn't consider long, I knew I had to hurry if I hoped to hear anything worth hearing. As I'd done with the coin, I tried to touch the box, only this time I tried hard to

---

make that touch feather light, and I didn't close my eyes. I matched what I saw with my eyes to the 'feel' of what was there inside my head. The second I caught what I imagined was the feel it, the edges began to buckle inward. I stopped right away, disappointed, but not surprised. I'd hoped that I might some day get to the point where I could use this without crushing the hell out of things, but it didn't look like that was going to be possible. Fortunately, crushing the hell out of something was what I needed this time.

The lid came up in two pieces. I reached in and drew out the nails carefully by the leather cord, fear, and a longing to see and speak to Ambrosine filling me. But as I took it out, something else caught my eye. The false bottom in the box had split. I moved the pieces out of the way and saw why the small box was so very heavy. Coins peeked up at me through a crack in the bottom. It looked like close to a hundred old coins of different sizes and makes, each with a small hole in it where it had once surely been on a chain. Having seen the video and seen Ophilia and Ursa and the red headed twins with coins, I could guess what these were. Dead ends. Or murders. Or suicides. Women who either couldn't bear a girl to carry on her line or were murdered after being taken by the Partan Priests for whatever crime, or found to be too weak in the power. Or women who died from disease or sickness, or whose children had, leaving no one to carry on with their coin.

I pushed the pieces back together and set the lid to right so no one would see, then turned and numbly tottered toward the door on my hurt feet.

"Ambrosine, come to me. Don't take me to you. I need you to come to me," I begged softly as I lifted the leather up and over my head and pulled the front of my shirt away to let the nails settle against the bare skin of my chest.

Nothing happened. No chill. No electric shock. No goosebumps. Zip.

I reached up and gripped the nails tightly and winced, but they were just cold metal in my hurt hand. Whatever spark of memory or magic they once held was gone now, or used up.

Maybe it had just been a memory?

The doubt niggled at me again, but then the throbbing pain in my feet and hand reminded me once again that I'd actually been there, or that a part of me had. Or that a part of me I didn't understand had made that memory real.

Frustrated and annoyed, and no longer caring if I got caught, I opened the door a crack and peeked out, eavesdropping the old fashioned way.

It was Delia and Carol, they held styrofoam cups in their hands and were taking slow steps as they strolled past my cracked open door, chatting happily. They'd clearly just come from lunch and it looked as if I'd missed my chance.

"It was a god awful way to live, but for its day the system was absolute genius, from the selection method and the testing down to the exclusion of non dominant units in the gene pool."

"Not just exclusion, elimination." Carol took a sip of her drink before continuing, the two getting farther away, heading down the hall. "Louis Partan clearly didn't want his genetic work slipping back into the general populace. Wicked smart, ruthless, and selfish just scratches the surface. That he joined in with the breeding from the beginning made the whole thing personal for him, and of course, he chose only the strongest women to breed with. Any children of his publicly married trophy wives were disposed of quietly, as a son of one of the witches was put in place to inherit the Duchy of Partan and carry on the line."

"I wish you wouldn't use that word," Delia scolded, stopping in the middle of the hall and putting her hands on her hips as she glared at Carol. "It's ugly. You'll alienate them further than you already have. You need to be more sensitive."

Carol stopped walking and turned to her accuser. I could see both their faces in profile, and Carol wasn't bothered in the least by the other woman's glare, which annoyed Delia. "They don't react negatively to being called witches, though I'd never call them that to their face, I've seen others do it and they ignore it. They don't recognize the word, or accept it. They see themselves as Prestonians. And they treat each other differently than they treat non Prestonians. And I'm not talking about trust, or the psychic communication, it's on a deeper level than that. Have you seen that blonde headed cook?"

Delia nodded grudgingly, "What's he, twenty?"

"And so pretty it's almost hard to look at him. We placed him there on purpose. He's not one of ours, if he were the mind readers would know inside of a second. He's just a pretty boy we placed there on purpose. He's tried every trick in the book for the past eight days to catch the eye of the girls and they won't even look at him. It's like they're a different species and they know it. Even Willow, when she was away from the Prestonians, instinctively developed an aversion to ordinary men that I believe she interpreted as being a sexual preference for women. And we know that she's protected her virtue with deadly violence. It's fascinating to think that behavior may be a genetically inherited predisposition. Her counselors from her old schools said that she was withdrawn and always seemed out of place or ill at ease in her surroundings. But here, she fits in wonderfully. And the girls accepted her even before that stigmata experience they forced onto her."

"I've watched the video four times. I'm not convinced it was forced."

"Perhaps not consciously, but as we saw with Willow in the liquor store and little Seraphina floating out of her sheets at night while she sleeps, these girls can do things unconsciously as well. Complicated and elaborate things. And the stigmata was definitely forced." Carol's tone was dogmatic. Decided. "Their world's crashing down. Their religious beliefs are being tested. They reached out with their powers blindly and forced this convenient oral prophecy of the end times and vengeance onto the girl who seemed to fit the mold."

"I'll have to watch it again, keeping in mind that incident in the liquor store. You make an interesting point." Delia sounded grudgingly convinced already. "As for the behavior of the Preston girls, they certainly don't behave like any group of human girls might under similar conditions," she laughed, a delighted, happy sound. "Genetically speaking, this is like finding the lost city of Atlantis with living inhabitants who all speak telepathically, or soon would have, if they had continued this process another few generations."

"Don't you think they will?"

"What? Continue?" Delia was shocked at the suggestion. "You mean go back to that barbaric lifestyle? How could you even suggest such a thing!?"

I watched as Carol smiled at Delia, her calm, teflon demeanor impervious to the other woman's outrage. If anything she seemed amused by it. "So quick to think the worst of me?" Carol shrugged, "We aren't the only ones contemplating these same questions. Before Willow threw her fit and ordered the sensitive ones to remove the listening devices and cameras, we overheard many of the girls worrying over what they would do when it came time to have children. Where they would come from and what they would do if they gave birth to a child that wasn't gifted, voiced, or even able to pass one of the tests."

"It's a valid question, but not one with any good answer," Delia grumbled.

"When they heard what was happening here with Willow, the older women and mothers flatly refused to believe it until some of their own daughters were allowed to contact them seeking mothers who would accept Willow as Ambrosine. Shortly after that, one of the mothers who were firmly against the idea shared the oral legend of Ambrosine Reborn with one of our counselors. According to the prophecy, Ambrosine Reborn had to be a virginal girl of the DeLaCroix line, one who held the nails and bore in her body the marks of Ambrosine. Apparently the stigmata event Willow endured was also forced on her grandmother and has been done to most of the women in the DeLaCroix line for hundreds of years. A type of self perpetuating prophecy."

"If that's so, and they are genuinely unaware that they forced this onto Willow, I can certainly see why the girls would believe she's Ambrosine Reborn." Delia said with feeling.

"If it stopped there, perhaps," Carol said sadly. "According to their prophecy, Ambrosine Reborn is to kill all the males of Preston for their sins and give blooded Partan coins to each girl, giving them her innocence and paying the debt they believe is owed the priests for saving their mothers during the witch trials. I'm sure Willow would gladly kill the older men with her bare hands if given a chance, but you've seen how she is with children. Her moral view is black and white with no gray. She'd die before she harmed a child, no matter who its father was."

"This oral prophecy didn't happen to mention how the women would get gifted children after the men were all dead?"

Carol nodded, "Our source believed they'd still become pregnant, even without the men."

"How so?"

"Spontaneous conception is not without precedence in history. It happened with a woman named Mary," Carol reminded.

"Good Lord! I'm surprised they left out walking on water and calling fire down from Heaven," Delia complained. "Once these girls see her as just Willow and not a savior we may have a mess on our hands."

I struggled to keep from freaking out as butterflies buzzed about inside my still delicate stomach, threatening to make me erupt again. Give them children! I might be a virgin, but I wasn't the Virgin Mary!

"I agree, and she may be a virgin, but she's not the Virgin Mary," Carol said this as if she'd overheard my thought and had mistaken it for her own. She paused for a confused moment before pressing ahead, "It will be messy once their fantasy crumbles."

"Hopefully this belief will simply wear thin over time," countered Delia, "if Willow doesn't end things sooner, which she may do once she hears what being 'Ambrosine' means to the other girls. If not, we'll have to wait and be patient until her own failures bring her back to reality. If it wouldn't be so incredibly disruptive I'd say removing her would be ideal, but as strong as she is, and with the others convinced she's their savior reborn.."

"They would fight, and that, we do not want," Carol said firmly.

Carol continued, but her voice sounded distracted. "Since I heard the girls worrying over where they'd get gifted children, I've been directing our geneticists to collect samples from the men in the event the women should decide to have no further contact with them."

"They cooperated?"

Carol laughed, "We threatened additional jail time, hinting strongly at the role reversal they would experience in prison from what they are accustomed to. After that pep talk, every last Preston man got with the program. With our help the Preston Girls will still have their children. I've also been assured the process can be manipulated so that any children they have will be female, carrying the genetic traits for the voice and telekinesis. The mother's genetics will still come into play but the male side of things will be assured..." her voice trailed off then started again. "Of course, making them aware of this has its own risks, since they may interpret our help as more evidence that the prophecy is real."

She sounded off. Funny. It felt as if she were looking for me. I peered through the crack and watched as she scanned up and down the hallway.

"What is it?" Delia asked.

"I don't know. I've got the strangest feeling I'm being watched."

"There's a camera at the end of the.."

"No! It's something else. Some one close by, a Preston Girl."

Now Delia laughed. "Are you saying you're getting a psychic impression Mrs. Rimes? They told me you were gifted in your own way, but I'm not seeing anyone out here in the hall. The only two unaccounted for are Mr. and Mrs. Opar, and who knows where they ran off to. And even if they were here they couldn't have gotten past security...."

I stepped back from the door.

"Is Willow awake?" I heard Carol ask, though she already knew I was somehow.

"I haven't been in to check on her yet, so she may be awake. We only gave her a small dose of Valium. We didn't want her to get upset at being drugged out for half the day. But she doesn't have the voice, and she's still bedridden."

When the door opened I was facing them from across the room, standing beside the box.

"Willow?" Delia said cautiously, as if she wasn't quite sure who I was.

"Ambrosine?" Carol asked, eyes pinned on the crushed box.

'She's wearing the nails,' the distinct murmur of Carol's thoughts opened this time, and I wasn't even trying to hear them. The words and meaning were just barely caught, but it surprised me so much I actually smiled at the hateful woman, then nodded, touching my chest where the nails rested.

Eyes wide, and clearly thrown by my smile, Carol sent a more deliberate sending that I also managed to hear now that I wasn't trying.

Shane Wesley Shelton

'Can you hear me Ambrosine?'

I nodded.

"Willow, are you alright?"

"Its Ambrosine," Carol voiced for Delia's benefit.

"That's quite a flip flop," Delia scowled, annoyed at not being a part of whatever was happening psychically that she was missing. "I thought you said it was a forced event? What is it now that makes you think she's, 'Ambrosine?'"

"Because Willow hates me, and this girl is smiling at me. And this girl has the voice, and Willow does not. Or didn't, until she put on the nails."

'Are you a ghost? A spirit trapped in the nails? Who are you?' Another deliberate sending, and though it was faint, I heard it again.

I made a face at that. Pretending I was Ambrosine was giving me the creeps. I let my expression drop into a dead eyed scowl.

"You said in vetro would work for us. Are you sure?" I asked, speaking out loud. Both women blinked in surprise.

'She heard it all then, or maybe not all…not about her father.' This nugget of a whisper from Carol's unguarded thoughts made my jaw drop open.

"What do you know about my father!?" I demanded.

"Get out of my head!" she shouted at me as she backed toward the door.

"Calm down Carol!" Delia ordered.

I mocked her distress. "Get over yourself Carol! It's okay to drug me and put May Green in my room, but you don't like being mind fucked yourself!" I gave her the finger, "Screw you! Now go run away and cry and come back when you're through freaking out, because we have business to discuss."

She already had the door open, but that last line caught her.

'Business?' she thought.

"Yes, business," I mocked out loud, but then thought better of it. "You know what. Go ahead and go, and stay gone this time. I want to talk to Senator Borden Reeves, not you."

Carol didn't like that idea. She stepped back into the room, shut the door, and started talking fast. "His name was Edmond Preston. The last of the Partan line. He was your father. He's dead. He died very young himself, in an ATV accident. You were his only gifted child."

The door opened a crack. "Willow! You shouldn't be up on your feet!" Dr. Doughtry pushed the door open and stepped into the room. He quickly retrieved the wheelchair from where it was parked and pushed it over. I dropped into it thankfully then spun myself around to face Carol.

"Who was Ambrosine?"

She narrowed her eyes. "What else did you hear?"

"You know something. Something other than their prophecy." It was an accusation, not a question. I felt she was holding something back.

"Yes, and no," she said, annoyed. "We've been translating the records brought over from France, though the only credible information we found so far was confirmation that Ambrosine did exist. A witch was brought in during the early years of the witch hunts with her name."

There was more. I could feel it.

"What else do you know?" I shouted.

"Please be calm, Willow." Delia knelt in front of my chair, eyes pleading. She pressed a hand to my forehead. "She's getting hotter," she told Daughtry.

Everet's digital voice crackled across the speakers, "Agent Rimes, she's dialed in and can feel that you're being less than forthcoming. It's upsetting her. Tell her the rest."

Past Dr. Daughtry and Delia, Carol was easing her way to the door Daughtry left open. The metal monstrosity they'd just installed swung shut in a blinding flash, connecting with the reinforced frame they'd installed with a bone jarring impact we felt in the floor, ceiling, and walls of the entire building. The three of us froze like statues, the only noise for a solid ten count was my panting breath and the echo of the boom as we waited to see what I might do next.

Worried faces peered through the small, shattered glass pane set into the door.

"Is everyone alright?" Everet's digital voice asked cautiously.

Though she'd been the one I almost cut in two, Carol was the first to find her voice.

"Another accident Willow?"

I glared to hide my fear, but my quavering voice gave me away. "You're not going anywhere until you tell me about Ambrosine." I didn't argue when Daughtry slipped the oxygen mask over my face. Vincent and those outside the door spoke to Carol on the intercom, then they got busy trying to open the door. When that didn't work they tried to bash it open, but unlike the wooden door, metal didn't bash easily. The door was bent and wedged tight inside the frame, sealing us in, and being sealed in wasn't sitting well with Carol. Her outsides looked annoyed, but her inside voice that skipped in and out like a distant radio station, was getting more frantic each minute.

After I had my breathing back to a more normal level, and was mostly over my own freak-out, I took off my mask and ordered Carol to tell me the rest of what she knew about Ambrosine.

"Open this door, then I'll tell you," she said as she paced back and forth in front of the door like a trapped animal.

"Karma's being a bitch to you today, isn't it?" I didn't say it meanly. It was more of a curious observation.

"What's that suppose to mean?" she stopped pacing to glare.

"You don't remember keeping me in a room for hours right after my concussion and nearly killing me to get the answers to your questions?"

"We didn't confine you! You could have left any time you wanted Willow!" she snapped.

I gaped at her, genuinely shocked, because I felt that she actually believed that. Her head seemed capable of justifying her actions again and again.

"Are you claustrophobic?" Dr. Daughtry eyed Carol with worry now and not me. "I can give you a shot of valium while we wait for them to get the door open."

"Perhaps Senator Reeves can tell me what you won't. Perhaps I'll also tell him I've been in your head, and that you're a sociopath. The only difference between us being, when I hurt someone, I own it, but you make excuses."

"Don't be cruel Willow," Delia scolded gently.

"It's alright Delia. This is how Willow reacts when she feels trapped." Carol pasted on a compassionate face, then gave me a congratulatory nod. "It's easy to forget what an exceptionally gifted manipulator you are," she said for the benefit of the others listening in on the intercom or trapped in the room with us. Carol was doing damage control. Trying to manipulate things herself.

She'd do whatever she had to do to stay on the team.

"Start talking about Ambrosine."

"Alright, Willow. I'll tell what pieces we know," Carol said, her voice placating and stripped of emotion as she fell into this role and tried to regain control. "The Partan Priests were fastidious about recording the family history of the women they brought in as part of their system for genetic breeding for specific traits, but when Ambrosine was taken she provided a very farfetched lineage. She claimed to be the great granddaughter of Pressyne. The same Pressyne who married the king of Scotland and bore three daughters, before she was seen doing magic in her garden and supposedly fled to the mystical Isle of Avalon with her children. One of her daughters, Melusina, later met and married a French noble. According to medieval folklore, Melusina was a fairy queen whose bottom half would turn either into a mermaid, or a serpent. Ambrosine claimed Melusina was her grandmother, though other historical records of the day credit the grandchild of Melusina as being a girl named Faustine. So she must have made this up. Even the Priests back then, when they did their research, came up with the same name, Faustine. They didn't believe her either."

My hands gripped the nails beneath my top as I tried to remember... the name. She'd been confused when I'd called her Ambrosine. I'd called her Ambrosine.

"What is it Willow?" Carol asked softly.

"Her name wasn't always Ambrosine." I said, speaking my thoughts out loud, my own mind whirling in crazy directions as I began to wonder if I'd inadvertently played some part in the start of this savior prophecy I was now trapped in.

"How do you know that wasn't always her name?" Carol asked, stepping closer.

I ignored her question and asked my own. "What else do you know about her?"

"Tell me!" I demanded when she hesitated.

"We know she was crucified, but according to what our linguists have been able to translate, she survived the burning because of a torrential downpour that put out the fire before she died. The townspeople were afraid that they'd angered God with what they'd done, so they took her in and nursed her back to health until the Priests of Partan came and took her away. According to the Priests own record, the villagers refused to accept the thirty coins they offered to pay, even when threatened with excommunication, insisting that Ambrosine had already paid for her sins. The priests still took her, but instead of a coin they used the nails she'd been crucified with as her token of debt, insisting that she still owed a debt to God for sparing her life, if not to them."

I remembered the flash of light. The storm. My hand tightened on the nails as if I could still feel them vibrating painfully in our bones.

"Was she struck by lightning?"

The chills that ripped through Carol were enough to make me look up and meet her wide open eyes. "The account called it a light from Heaven." She took a step closer and knelt in front of my chair as Delia and Dr. Doughtry watched, silent and wide eyed. "Were you there Willow, with her? Are you there with her now?"

I blinked at her. Did she think I was in two places at once? I did feel outside myself and floating, though I sat in a wheelchair. Was it the drugs, my messed up head, or was it something else making me feel this way? For the first time since I met her, I actually looked at Carol. Delia had called her 'gifted'. I could hear her voice in my head. And I'd traveled back to her past, like I had with Ambrosine. I compared the feel of that girl I'd been inside of in the past to the hungry look deep down in the eyes of the woman who knelt before me. Not much had changed. Always feeling 'not part of the group', and doing horrible things to be included. Always looking and never finding. Until I came here, I guess I was the same, only I didn't do horrible things 'too' fit in, I did them because I didn't. She may have been my opposite in that way, but in another way we were the same.

I reached out and touched her face and she flinched, as if expecting a blow. She blushed in embarrassment at her own fear as I studied her. She was actually pretty when she wasn't trying to kill me, and so very lost.

"Hello little witch." I smiled at her again, but this time I meant it. She seemed transfixed by my gaze. "If you were alive when she was, you would have burned with us. Or been taken by the priests." I released her from my gaze, leaning back in the chair, closing my eyes. "When the priests took her, did she live?"

"Yes. She lived with the Priests twelve years before she died. Her three female children possessed the gift, two of which survived to bear children of their own. The priests gave Ambrosine a last name because she only had a first name, and all their women had surnames that they handed down to their daughters." Almost reverently Carol said, "Ambrosine DeLaCroix. Ambrosine 'of the cross'. You are her child Willow. And if the rest of the account was true, that means you are also the child of kings and fairy queens."

I began weeping as I sat there in my chair, contemplating the horror of what I'd done. All I'd done for Ambrosine had been to steal her from a merciful hell on the cross just to deliver her to a different kind of hell. I should have let her burn. I should have burned with her! The child of kings and the daughter of a fairy queen deserved better, but because of me she'd been raped for twelve years by the Priests of Partan.

All because I saved her.

The vision of Mel and Mr. Ronicker flashed in my head and my stomach churned while Dr. Daurghty and Delia fluttered about, asking me again and again what was wrong. Daughtry went and got his needle ready. The drugs were on their way.

The horrible, biting sound of metal on metal shocked me from the spiraling abyss of my own dark thoughts and made me look up, gritting my teeth against the noise. They were trying to cut through the door.

The sound was godawful. I wanted it to stop! I had to make it stop!

I reached out, but not with my hand - but with my mind. As soon as I felt the top and bottom edges the door it began to buckle in on itself from the middle. Out in the hall men shouted in alarm as the door continued to bend double, metal straps stretching from the new stainless steel hinges like pulled bubble gum. I gritted my teeth and squeezed harder, pouring all my rage at what I'd done and what had been done 'to her' into that unseen hand. The horrible sound of the saw was gone, but now the metal itself screamed out as if in pain while it crumpled into an ever tighter, smaller ball within my invisible fist. I closed my eyes and screamed with the door, sharing our pain until darkness found me.

Ambrosine Reborn

I was still in bed three days later, awake, but withdrawn. My eyes were closed and I was pretending it was all a dream as Nurse Bell and her four, young helpers came in and started to work on my bandages. I stayed in my shell, only dimly aware when the hanging strings of beads that had replaced my door began to make a racket as a people entered my room. I felt them more than saw them, as their presence found my mind. It was Preston women. Not five or ten, but dozens, and they kept coming and coming, ignoring Bell's complaints. I felt the air thicken in the room as they packed the space, all of them whispering to one another about my hands and feet and the nails that lay on my chest. I heard the older voices of mothers and younger voices that I'd not heard before. I even heard grandmothers who'd been included as part of whatever this was that Ursa had cooked up.

Was this her idea of an intervention?

Who knew.

Whatever.

I tried to drift inside myself. The spoken words around me I was able to tune out, but those shared by the voice as they talked back and forth around me and about me I couldn't hide from. The soft murmurs in my head that sometimes became words pierced my protective shroud, and despite my best efforts, I pieced together that some of these new girls and women were from families who'd fled before the round up. They'd gathered together at a ranch in Wyoming, only to be found again and rounded up there. Others were the older girls and mothers that had been held nearby, but apart from us. They all stayed in the room, watching and talking silently as Bell and her group of young helpers continued their work on my bandages as if they were still alone.

'Ursa, why is she open and exposed like this? Hasn't anyone told her how to close her mind?' asked one older woman of Ursa with the voice. Other older voices in the room murmured the same question, equally offended and even scandalized on my behalf as if I were naked and indecent.

"Once someone starts to shield they begin to do it even when they sleep, and what she's seen and who she is belongs to all of us," Ursa said out loud, her voice defensive. "And at first we didn't even know ourselves, so all we could do was listen, and wait, and see."

"And what exactly is it that you think you now know?" grumbled one of the older mothers in the back out loud, though others quickly put her in her place.

'If she doesn't care that we can all see her, she can at least show us how it happened. Ursa's right, we all need to see it!' a powerful young 'voice' declared, her sending so crystal clear I knew she wasn't merely talking over my head, but meant me and every woman here to hear it. 'I need to see it! How else will we know she didn't drive the nails into her own hands and feet, or have you do it?' She and Ursa argued back and forth with the voice, then the older women joined in, ganging up on Ursa and the other girls who'd been with me from the beginning.

'What of the rest of the prophecy?' one of the mothers asked, also broadcasting and speaking to the group, but unlike the teenager girl her voice wasn't mocking or flip, but sounded sincere in my head. 'She's brought an end to our way of life, but she's not ended all the priests and given us vengeance as the prophecy says. I will accept that they can give us gifted children through in vitro. And I accept that she's pure and untouched, and I accept that she truly bears the marks and the nails for I've already seen your memories of that, but where are the blooded coins? Either the prophecy is real or it's not real Ursa, we can't live in halves. The coins were the heart of the prophecy. They were supposed to free us of the curse, and her blood was to pay the price for our sins.'

A fogy vision like a dream was there in my head, as if I were seeing out of someone else's eyes in the room. The angle was lower and close to my bedside. The mother who was speaking was close by. She was shorter, and was looking up at Ursa, eyeing the chain around her neck.

"You have your mothers coin, you can at least dip it in her blood if you believe in her so much, but where will I and my four daughters get our coins?'

Anger and frustration touched my heart. Whoever I was in felt sad and hopeless too, hopeless because she did not have her own coin. I think it was Daphne.

"Some girls have two or three," I recognized Viki's voice as she argued out loud. "They can share. Or we can make more."

"It has to be a coin of Partan, not just any coin," the mother said firmly. "And they stopped giving them out a hundred years ago when they ran out of the old cursed coins, and the high priesthood ended with Edmond's death, so even if they did wish to make more, they can't." She'd spoken out loud to Vicki, but then she spoke directly to me with the voice, but instead of looking down at where I lay she looked down and into the eyes of the girl I peered out of. 'I can't accept you DeLaCroix, or be a part of this when there is no hope for my children. What would be the point? I'm sorry for all of us.'

I finally opened my eyes and studied her for myself. Her dirty blonde hair looked flat and haggard. Bright hazel eyes that looked hurt. Mouth turned down, but set in what was a beautiful, forty year old face. And she cared about her daughters. I lost one brief moment as I looked at her, wishing she'd been my mother.

She gave me a sympathetic look, but not one that softened her resolve.

"What will you do without the coins? How will you live without the legend of your bloody, savior Ambrosine Reborn?"

She cast a cautionary glance at Nurse Bell, who was in the room but pushed back against the wall, then back at Carol and Vincent, who lingered in the open doorway. Behind them were other faces I didn't recognize, more of the Preston women and mothers. She turned back to me, but spoke with the voice so those watchers did not hear but the Preston women could. 'I'll say whatever I have to say, and do whatever I must to keep my children with me, then we'll go back to the ranch and wait for my husband or some of the other men to be freed. I want gifted children, and I must have a strong man to have them. And even if they could do in vetro like they told us on the way here, I and my daughters are still bound by the curse. They tell me that some of the girls here already suffer with the fever. They said that you've had the fever, too. That's the curse at work child. As much as I hate it and wish it wasn't so, eventually we'll all sicken and die without being sanctified. Either there is a reason for all the hell we've endured, or I should kill myself right now.'

I could feel it. She would do exactly what she said.

Shane Wesley Shelton

"You bitch," I said softly, sick at heart and resigned. "Why won't you people leave me be," I complained wearily.

There was no hiding. No dreaming this away.

I turned my head and looked toward the window ledge, and the box.

"Did that little tramp just call you a.."

"Hush Candis!" she snapped at the smaller version of herself at her side as she studied me with surprised eyes. 'Use your gift and listen!' she ordered her outraged daughter. 'Listen!'

I waited patiently as they and the others in the room did just that. Eventually they cleared a hole for me to see the box. Trying to be as gentle as possible, I grabbed the thing 'without hands'. The antique box splintered even more as it lifted up into the air. The room was silent as it glided across the room. I let go when it was over my bed and dumped the broken ruin of the box and its hidden contents right into my lap. Ancient French, German and English coins glittered in the fluorescent lighting, the crude holes bored into the metal looked to have been made with ancient tools. Women and girls started to weep or drop to their knees in fits of religious ecstasy, though there wasn't much of that because it was standing room only.

'There's a big plastic container in the bathroom - bring it,' I thought. The bathroom was already open with women using that extra space to stand in. One of the mothers already in the bathroom, handed it to another who passed it along until it was at my side.

'Daf, honey,' I thought to my little helper pressed tight to the bedsides, 'you girls gather the coins.'

I turned to Nurse Bell and motioned her over as little hands with big, wide open eyes obediently set to work on their precious treasure hunt, picking through the splintered box and searching the folds of my sheets for coins.

The women made a hole and Bell approached my bedside cautiously.

"Please draw some blood."

She turned and glared through the faces and over their heads at Vincent. "Are you going to let her do this? This is insane!"

He didn't enter the over crowded room, but spoke from the doorway. "If these women were from an isolated tribe in New Guinea and had an unusual religious belief or custom, we would respect it, even if we thought it was sad, pointless, illogical, and even harmful - to a point," he said firmly, indicating there were limits to what he would allow us to do. "Legally and morally we would be in the wrong to interfere. And we may not be gifted like they are, but we are observant. Willow is doing what she feels she must, what's best for the group, even if that's not what's best for her. And I believe she intends to do this with or without our help, so please make her choice as painless and as safe as possible Bell."

He seemed reluctant to intrude, yet utterly unable to keep from asking at least one question, "Willow, forgive me, but in your vision of the past, did you tell Faustine, or Ambrosine, to put the coins in the box?"

The women had leaned to each side so I could see him and he me.

I shook my head no.

"She had the voice," Carol said quickly, "You must have thought of them while you were inside her, and she knew to put the coins inside the box from that memory."

I raised my bandage free hands, exposed palms facing her, "We were being crucified. She was thinking of Sibyla and I was thinking about murdering the hammer man, not coins." Nurse Bell reached over and grabbed one of my wrists carefully and pulled out her watch to check my pulse, then frowned.

"She's in no condition to give blood to anyone. And she has a fever."

I'd seen her draw my blood often enough. I thought about where the needles and things were and the mothers in the room went to those shelves and began to pull out what they needed. Nurse Bell looked like she wanted to curse, but she pushed through to the cabinets and took over as the women watched what she was doing with suspicious eyes. I told Ursa to collect everyone's coins, then to take the bin out and collect every coin from all the girls here.

"I'm only doing this shit once, so they all go in now," I said out loud, eyeing Viki as she gripped her own coin protectively, eyes wild as she eyed the bin Ursa held. Her coin was precious. It was the most valuable thing she owned or ever would own, a family heirloom, passed down for generations. I'd seen how the girls with coins had strutted around with a sense of entitlement, and I'd also noticed the longing looks of the others who had no coin every time one of them pulled it out to flash it about.

Around me in the room mothers and daughters watched, many nodding grimly in agreement with my thoughts, others who had coins looked embarrassed or even ashamed.

"We are all the same family," I reminded Viki, and the others. "You can keep the one you have if you want, but don't ask me for one with my blood on it if you do." My eyes and heart held no mercy. None.

She couldn't get it off fast enough. Her coin went into the bin.

An old woman with silver gray hair cackled like a witch, though she smiled like a little girl. I watched as she took her own coin off the chain around her neck and dropped it into the bin.

Ten minutes later Ursa returned, the bin heavy with coins. I no longer needed to give instructions, as the women and girls took over. Nurse Bell was asked to leave. The IV bag, filled with my blood was dumped in the bin and mixed with the coins by one of the mothers who was wearing white gloves. I watched her kneading the bloody mess like a devil's brew while being careful not to touch the blood herself, as if my blood were even more precious than the coins. Ursa had me leave my hands and feet unwrapped so the wounds showed. The mothers got me out of bed and put me in a wheel chair, then rolled me out to the commons where all the Preston Girls and all the newly arrived mothers and grandmothers had gathered in a circle. Our seventy had grown to over two hundred. Among the new faces in this crowd I saw one I recognized. The cold eyes the ex-police woman looked at my hands and feet. She dropped to her knees, her voice in my head begging Ambrosine's forgiveness.

Ursa took charge, calling on the old woman who'd laughed in my room, telling her to tell the history of the curse. Light headed from blood loss and sickened by what I was hearing, I waited until it was over and Ursa sent out the first girl. She was a serious eyed, grave faced two and a half year old named Abby who'd been among the youngest of the girls we'd had with us. She walked away from what had to be her own mother who she'd been reunited with. She'd enjoyed my ready lap on more than a few occasions, but this time she stopped short and stood before me, expectantly.

"What do you want?" I asked, wondering if she understood what she was doing.

She gave me a curious look.

"One of your coins. One with your blood." She answered with the honest and simple logic of a child, but with the serious need of an adult.

"Why do you want my bloody coin?"

"To break my curse."

With tears clouding my vision, thinking the whole world had gone insane and me along with it, I turned to the bloody coins. It felt as if I were falling down the rabbit hole as I leaned over and reached into the bin. I dug down into the wet sticky mess for one stuck stubbornly to the bottom, as if it might be more magical than one on the top. My hand came up dripping blood, one red coin pinned between forefinger and thumb. Weeping as I fell ever farther into Neverland, I put the coin into her tiny, open palm then leaned forward and kissed her on the forehead. On a mad whim, I painted a bloody, upside down cross on her forehead with my fingertip.

"Your curse is broken Child of Ambrosine," I told her, then sent her away with her bloody coin and cross marked brow.

As soon as she walked away the next girl stood before me expectantly. 'Ask me', she spoke in my head. So I did. The pattern was set, from the children to the older girls and women. They wanted the ceremony, the trappings. I gave them that and all my tears until I was cried out and wrung out and the last woman had a coin, felt the press of my lips to her forehead, and the tightness of drying blood on her brow.

Mrs. Opar

Sarah Lavonia Opar had circled around all the old haunts for days until she'd caught sight of her husband at an out of the way business, Milton Propane and Kerosene. Milton was the only 'Non Preston' man she'd ever seen her husband talk to, and even then it was only to make small talk as he filled the propane tank at the house three times a year. Of course, her husband saw her at the same time she spotted him. Right away he headed toward her car. Not quite sure what to do, Sarah fell into the old habit of submission. She parked and turned off the motor, then waited with her hands in her lap, eyes down until he opened the passenger side door and climbed inside.

Wade eyed her hard for a minute, seeking any type of fight he might need to knock out of her, then asked if she had anything to eat. Sarah got out, opened the trunk and made sandwiches and listened, as Milton and her husband talked about a Ranch in Wyoming where some of the families had been before they'd been taken away.

"Well, I guess it's over then. I mean, really OVER," Milton said, looking a bit uncomfortable as he leaned against the old Buick she'd pulled up in.

Wade just glared at the man as he pushed the sandwich Sarah made into his mouth and chewed.

Now that Sarah was here, Milt risked the question he'd been wanting to ask.

"Did you really do all that shit to Mel that they're saying on the news? I mean, you wouldn't share out your own daughter to half the town. You wouldn't," a sick expression stuck on Milt's face.

Sarah practically stopped breathing. She watched as Wade swallowed, then smiled. Then laughed.

"Geez Milton," he shook his head, "I ain't gonna lie, some families did that sharing around, but not us. We ain't that kind."

Milton nodded. Mumbled "Good" a few times, stuck his hat back on and said his goodnights. He didn't get three steps before Wade was on him, raining down blows until their wasn't a reason to keep hitting a dead man.

Sarah watched as her husband rummaged through his pockets and came out with keys. He coughed as he went over and got into one of the delivery trucks and backed it up to one of the big, metal storage tanks. She watches as he turned on the pump and filled the truck with kerosene.

"What are we gonna do now, Wade?" She found the courage to ask, watching as he disconnected the hose, rolled it up and stowed the thing on the side of the truck.

"I'm the last of the Partan Priests not rotting in jail," he said with no small amount of pride as he tied the hose down. "It was our sworn duty to keep you women in your place and keep you from evil. You're all nothing but witches, and I won't - I CAN'T - let the world be tainted with that evil!" He growled darkly, then coughed again. He paused to catch his breath.

"You mean to burn'em up then? All the Preston Girls?"

"I have to," he panted as he leaned against the side of the truck.

"Your own daughter? Me, too?"

Wade dropped to his knees.

Sarah slipped inside the car and locked the door and watched from the other side of the glass as her husband finished dying. But as she sat there, she couldn't help but think and worry. Try as she might, in the end there was only one way to be sure Mel would stay safe. Only one way to help that wild girl fulfill the prophecy. Only one way to be anything more than a monster of a mother and a failure in life. One way.

And what better way for a witch to die, than to burn.

Burning Day

They were calling what we'd done that day, 'The Breaking'. One of the girls, no one knew who, circulated the rumor that they had to wear the bloody cross on their brow for three days before they could wash, and take it off. The others liked the idea, so that became the way things were. They'd taken pictures during the ceremony of each girl receiving her coin, and I'd overheard mothers and girls that night, before they took me to bed, already pestering the staff to have those pictures blown up and framed. Today those photos were already back, blown up and framed as requested. Vincent had brought in a jeweler who'd set up his little work station in the commons. I saw the long line of smiling girls waiting to have their coins put onto nice, new chains. I watched as the man worked with nervous eyes and tight smiles for the girls and women with upside down crosses marked in blood across their brows.

I was enjoying the busy noise of the girls in the commons, parked out in the middle of the room and resting my eyes in the chair when Vincent and Carol began to call for everyone to gather in the commons, though keeping a secret was a moot point because others had already heard what they wanted to share in their heads.

"They're dead! All the men are dead!" the calls rang out.

"They burned to death like witches on the cross! Mel's mother killed them all!"

Girls and women all across the room began to fall to their knees, raising their hands and crying out "Ambrosine!" like zealots. Others shouted viciously that, "'The Day of Vengence' had come at last!"

We still gathered in the commons and listened, as a grave faced Everet shared the details not already mugged from his head, and there were tears, but not many, a sniffle or two from the youngest girls whose fathers hand not yet become monsters in their eyes, a tear or two from the young married women, not a drop from the few gray heads among us. Everet pressed hard for some show of compassion on behalf of the children and young Preston boys, as well as the sixty guards, doctors and other social workers who'd died in the blaze, but he could tell this was not the place to seek solace for counterparts he may have known and cared for. The only

---

true concern the women had was for the 'genetic material' Carol had been collecting from the Preston men to ensure their continued ability to bear gifted children. They listened in anxious silence until hearing that those 'materials' had been stored in another location and were 'safe'.

It wasn't truly celebration that rolled around the room, but a crisp sense of finality, completion, and over it all a creepy vibe that it was all true. Every bit. The curse, the prophecy, the coins, and even me. Especially Ambrosine. I saw the unsettled look on Vincent's face as he glanced my way, then excused himself from the room. I saw the fearful looks of the guards who had to stay. Men who seemed less glad to be here with us than they had moments before. Here with witches. Real witches. Real curses. Real death. I listened to the banter of the women, voices in and outside my head merging in and out as if I now existed in both a dream land and the real world. 'Burning Day' became the hot title tossed around for the day's event. Breaking Day, and now Burning Day. Our first witch holidays, I laughed as the thought struck me funny. How sweet. Not a duck, or a goose, or a ham... meatloaf? Burt meatloaf! With lots of ketchup! I laughed. Their worried eyes were on me, and the presence of so many was there in my head, all of them listening to my idle thought. A broader circle of space formed around me as they gave me a place to freak out, drift in the tide, or whatever, while still able to see me, hear me, and know I was there. Nurse Bell came and tried to take me back to my room, but I didn't want to be alone. They told her what I wanted, then sent her away. I stayed in my chair in the middle of the commons as the women moved around me. Lived around me. Talked about me.

I sat there doing the same, living my own life in my head, remembering the ugly call I'd made to Mrs. Opar and wondering if I'd somehow pushed her to do this. Had I, yet again, been the instrument of prophecy? The straw that broke the camel's back? The pebble in a pond six hundred years ago that became the tidal wave of today? I knew that even as I had them, my fears that I'd been responsible were being heard, and that all my matching doubts were also being heard, then discounted, as these women decided for themselves what to believe.

Burning Day passed like a waking dream. One I didn't remember ending.

Waking Up

Ursa and Ophilia were still more or less in charge of me, but Mrs. Roule, one of the mother's who'd worked as a nurse, had taken over my care in most ways. She came to my room to fetch me this morning with Ursa and Ophilia, but she'd clearly stiffened the girls spines because they flat out refused to let me use the chair and ignored my begging. They made me use my feet and walk. They did at least let me hold onto my favorite, pretty helper for support as I made my way into the commons again, though for the life of me I didn't remember ever leaving there last night. When I hobbled out into the room I had to stop and take it all in for a moment. The place was transformed. So many more women, and so many more helpers. So much activity! And it looked like Delia, or Vincent, or someone had gotten organized finally. All the workers were now dressed in matching prim white uniforms, name tags in place, all with happy smiles on their face and busy about whatever they were up to as they moved amongst the women and girls.

Holly sat me at a table with Vincent, Carol and two doctor ladies in white lab coats. One was young and pretty. She was foreign, perhaps from India. Her name tag read Aashi Poddar. I smiled at the pretty name and at the pretty girl who returned the smile warmly, but not in a way that was an invitation. The other was a plump, older blonde who did not have a name badge. There were old coffee and drink cups sitting on the table. Folders and notebooks, Ipads and a laptop strewn about. I could tell they'd been at it for a while. What I was about to receive was a summery. Decisions had already been made.

Girls and mothers around me listening in to my wave length looked a bit uneasy, but they didn't look away from me either. One of them gave the plump, nameless woman a nod.

"We believe we know what's causing the fevers, and we also believe we know how to make them stop," she said firmly.

'And...'

"She said 'And'," one of the mothers put my thoughts to spoken words.

"So tell her!" another ordered roughly.

The woman pouted, but complied. "After passing one of the three initial tests, the Priests of Parton absolutely forbid the use of what they called 'the way', and 'the voice', calling their use a sin. Though women being women, and talking mind to mind being undetectable by the men, the voice was still used, but not the way. We've been able to determine, and verify through their records, that all the girls with the fever have had at least some ability with telekinesis, what you call 'the way'. By not using this ability we believe potential energy within their system eventually builds up and that this is what causes the fevers."

"But what does that have to do with being raped by the Preston men?" I asked, interested enough to talk for myself.

"Nothing," she said bluntly.

Aashi and Carol gave the woman a reproachful look. "The placebo effect was in play. They were told that it would help with the fevers, and they believed it, so it did. And rape was also trauma," Aashi said firmly, her voice nicely accented by her country of origin. "Trauma, and even torture can shock the system and relieve stress, or at least replace one type of stress for another, and as much as I hate that it was forced, sex in itself is a natural stress reliever. So I believe there was some value to what was done beyond the placebo effect. Some," she said, "but it is not the best way. Many girls still died of fever, even after being sanctified repeatedly by many men." She was clearly disgusted by the idea.

"The greater the gift, the higher the chance the fevers will be a problem," added the other woman as she eyed me with what looked like worry.

"Ambrosine has a fever right now," Holly announced unexpectedly. And then the mother hens were on me.

After much arguing, I agreed to 'practice' using my gift, but not inside the building. They put me back in my wheelchair, but before we went outside Carol and Everet took me to one of the recently cleared out rooms that they'd filled with desks and chairs, and what they called 'games'. Women in white uniforms holding digital pads smiled as they walked amongst the rows, charting progress and making notes, even offering encouragements to the young girls and older women as well. I noticed that all the women and girls in the room had white wrist bands.

One of the white wearing helpers greeted us at the door.

"Name?" she asked as she looked at Holly, who was pushing me, and then down at me. "I'll register you."

Carol explained the process. "In order to see if this works as a cure for the fevers, we have to record how long each girl spends in practice and track each girls progress and strength, and track their change in temperature over time. We plan to do that with these games, and other games that are being designed, and with the arm bands that monitor temperature."

"Would you like to play?" The girl in white asked Holly sweetly.

'Wow, she's a cute one.'

I blinked at hearing the idle thought of this smiling girl who was eyeing my favorite helper.

Holly looked down to me and gave me a reassuring smile and I nodded distractedly, because I wanted to see.

"Holly Doutch." she gave her name.

The woman entered her into the pad, asking other questions as she did so, though I could see that as soon as she entered Holly's name a veritable smorgasbord of information was already there on the screen, at her fingertips. She produced a wrist band and turned it on. Holly's temperature appeared on the digital screen.

"And your name?" she asked me.

I looked over at Carol and Vincent who just stared back, waiting to see what name I would give. Across the room other girls stopped what they were doing and half stood in their chairs to watch.

I looked at the oblivious girl that had to be brand new and gave her my name. "Ambrosine DeLaCroix," and watched her go pale. Carol took the frightened girls pad, entered me into the system and gave me my own band. I sighed at the sight of 101.2 degrees on the readout.

"We've just begun this process Ambrosine," Carol addressed me by my new name for the first time as I scowled down at the glowing numbers on my wrist band. "These games are crude, and the tracking data and all of our early research and testing is just now being broken down, but it already looks promising. Please try not to worry too much. We think this will work."

She turned and led the way down the row, but I felt her doubts. Something was off in her promise. Holly pushed me over to the table Carol stopped in front of. On the table was nothing but a candle, but in front and set into the table itself of was a digital pad.

Across the top of the pad the text 'Welcome!' flashed on and off.

'Hello there Holly, thanks for coming to light my fire.'

Geez, was everyone after my girl today? What the fuck!?

I blushed and squirmed in my chair as Holly, Mrs. Roule and others behind me laughed. The flashing greeting vanished and an old fashioned stop watch took its place at the top of the screen, making this candle lighting game into a timed race.

The bottom half of the screen had two buttons.

'Press here when you're ready to start.' A green button.

'Press here when you've lit the candle.' A red button.

It made sense to me in a way, even if it was a bit creepy. It was a way to encourage them to 'push' themselves. To try harder. To go faster. Reach farther. And a way to wear them out and use up that dangerous energy.

"I might not be able to do it. I only did a candle once before," Holly offered her disclaimer shyly as she took her seat.

Other girls left their games and gathered around, watching, adding additional pressure. Even so, after two minutes the wick flickered to life. The candle was lit. Smiling, Holly pressed the red button on the pad.

"Let's see how fast Ambrosine can do it," Emily, one of the girls from the room I used to share snarked wickedly, pouring cold water on Holly's accomplishment and vanquishing the beautiful smile I'd been enjoying. Emily's wicked grin had already vanished by the time I looked up. Her eyes were already pooling with unshed tears.

Why did she do this to herself?

I sighed, turned my chair then reached down and put the brakes on and stood up and faced a shamed faced Emily. Everyone watched expectantly as I reached my arms around the poor, mean girl and gave her a great big hug. I held onto her as she cried for just a bit, giving what comfort I could and enjoying the hug myself. When I pulled away enough to see her face, my wrist band beeped. She held no thought for the tears on her own face as she looked down at my monitor. 101.3, temperature rising.

She cast desperate eyes at Carol. "She's so hot!"

"We're taking her downstairs now," Carol assured her.

"Why downstairs?" asked one of the new mothers suspiciously. "What's wrong with her working with us right here?"

"Because she's too strong," one of the others answered out loud, broadcasting the vision of me mangling the metal door of my room.

"That's impossible!" The woman gaped at me, the bloody cross I'd painted on her forehead still easily visible.

'We told you she was Ambrosine!' Someone from the room broadcast with the voice loudly and the woman flinched as if the rebuke had stung. The oblivious helpers wearing white all shot me fearful looks as if I'd done something to the woman.

"Please, don't let her get sick," Emily wept, pushing forward and hugging me again fiercely and pinning Carol with her imploring gaze. I soothed and comforted, and told her I'd be okay, but all Carol gave was a tight smile as she removed Emily and put me back in my chair, then gathered up my little group of keepers, and her own cloud of watchers and guided the whole caravan toward the elevator.

As I rolled down the hall, I did some thinking. Maybe it was Carol's coldness to Emily's heartache, but I felt that something else was off with her. Something bigger. Elusive. As they pushed me into the elevator, I remembered something I'd tried to forget on purpose. Tried, because I knew there was good in her. But good or not, Carol was weak. Weak and easily swayed, and when it came right down to it, it would only be crocodile tears that fell if she hurt me. Carol wanted to be part of the team. But, not my team, their team. Then I realized something else even more troubling, not about her, but about myself.

I'd been walking around in a haze, letting things happen.

Easy prey.

I thought back on all the extra nurses and helpers I'd seen today, but also all the extra guards - standing in doorways, along the halls, at the elevator as we got in - watching. A deja-vu moment married the scene in my head to walking down the halls of Preston High, big beefy men lining the walls and lurking in doorways. That scene merged again into one of muggy faced villagers, wild eye'd priests, and the long filthy face of the hammer man, all of them surrounding me. All of them watching. Some of them were probably even good people, but that didn't change what was what.

With grim certainty I knew that I had to wake up. Stop dreaming. Stop denying what I was.

So I was a witch! So what!

So I was Ambrosine Reborn! So what!

So I'd saved myself and the others from the men of Preston. So what!

What I'd done yesterday would not save me, or them, from the monsters lining our walls today. I had to wake up. To take control and own this! Eat or be eaten. Be easy prey, or out monster the monsters.

"What is it? What's wrong?" Carol asked, looking from face to face, having sensed the change of mood in myself and the Preston girls and women, who'd all gone stone still and deathly silent.

As the elevator doors opened, I found myself thinking about the thought that had just run through my head. There were no more Preston men. They were dead. So were they really 'Preston Girls' anymore. And if they weren't, then what were they?

Ambrosine's children. Ambrosinians? Ambrose Girls? My girls.

"Will someone tell me what's wrong?" a voice buzzed in the background.

Were they my children then? Was I in some way their mother?

I thought about my mother and Aunt Fay as Carol glared at me and the others. Fay had abandoned the Preston Girls and tried to live a life in the modern world. And she'd tried to have my mother abort me and kill me. And my mother had simply crumpled in on herself and been too weak. In the end she'd tried to kill me over a broken bottle of booze.

'We are not going ANYWHERE until you tell me what's wrong!' Carol's direct sending rudely pushed through all my own thoughts.

I looked up at her and sent back just as forcefully, 'My mother was a good person at times, but she loved alcohol more than me. And you're a good person too most of the time, but you love 'them' more than you'll ever love me. I was thinking that your just like my mother.'

"Can we go now?" I said out loud. "Because I have work to do."

I gave her a second then gave a face to match the ugly one she was giving me, "Shit Carol, you did ask what was wrong? Don't play in the kitchen if you can't take the heat."

'Heat. Yeah. Whatever,' Carol thought as she looked down to my wrist band, then turned and walked away.

'As strong as she is, she'll probably die of the fever in a few weeks.' I wasn't sure I'd heard it, but from the way Holly's grip turned white knuckle tight on the handles of my chair, I guess I had.

As Holly pushed me along behind Carol, I came to one solid conclusion. After I worked my ass until I couldn't crush a marshmallow with my mind I was going to go upstairs and start shamelessly hitting on girls till I found at least one who wouldn't mind some quality time with a gay girl.

I wanted to live!

Not Gemma, unless she needed the help for her own fever. She reminds me too much of Sibyla, and I want something new, not a ghost of the past that would steal from what I did today and mess with my mind. Not Ursa, you're in charge in a way and that would be awkward, even though you're crazy hot.

Behind me somewhere she laughed.

I knew she was listening, they were all listening. I continued my list.

Then there's Tazy, the blind girl.. she gives me goose bumps and chills, but I think she kinda likes the other blind girl already, but that was just a guess.

'Holly?' a voice spoke into my head...

Had Holly said that?! Her voice inside my head was soft and breathy like her spoken voice, but this was deeper, more like my own.

Was she trying to slip herself into my list?

I tried to think of a white sheet of paper and not the pretty eyes over me, or what thoughts were going through her head as my mouth went dry. I tried not to notice the long blond hair at the edges of my vision as she leaned over the chair. Tried not to think about why she was always the first one at my door, ready to take care of me. Why she smiled at me the way she did. Or when they asked me who I wanted to come take care of me, why I didn't ask for the others on my 'list', not even Gemma, but always asked for Holly.

"That's an unusual expression." Carol had stopped to face me again at the last set of doors leading outside. "Are you sure you feel up to this Ambrosine? Perhaps you should go up and lay down for a while?"

All the voiced women and girls with me began laughing and laughing as Holly and I turned into living tomatoes while Carol cursed, inside and outside her head, demanding to know what was so damn funny.

Other Books
By Shane W. Shelton and
Believing Magic Books

Believing Magic Series:

Believing Magic
Kingdom Come
Sacrifice
Garden of Wrath
All Around the Throne
Devil's Tithe

∞

Everything Series:
The Gift | Everything

∞

The Traverler Series:
Midori | Mims | Meila

Stand Alone Singles:
Beyond The Edge
Melina May
Cinderella, Cinderella
Frank Dobbs and the OtherLands
A Girl Called Grace

For news on upcoming release dates visit:
www.believingmagic.com